"What're you looking for?"

Cole turned his gaze to the sky. "We can't go much farther before it gets totally dark, so I'm looking for an alternative to sleeping under the stars tonight."

"What do you have in mind?"

After taking off his hat, he glanced at Serena, then back to the map. A lock of hair hung over his forehead, and he reminded her of the boy she used to know. Her heart warmed at the endearing image. *If only...*

The thought was ridiculous. He wasn't that boy and she wasn't the girl she'd been, either. Too much had happened to ever repair the damage.

Dear Reader,

Welcome to Spirit Creek, Arizona. I'm delighted to spend more time in the picturesque fictional town that was also the setting for my last book. When I wrote *The Mistake She Made,* I knew Serena Matlock would get her own story–because after all the years she's spent watching out for her twin brother after the accident the night of their high-school graduation, she was due for a little happiness. I discovered all too quickly, however, that her happiness wouldn't come easily.

Writing Serena's story hasn't been easy, either. It hasn't been easy because Serena has such a complicated background and her relationships with the people involved in her life are extremely complex. As a writer, I hate to torture my heroines and heroes, but I soon discovered it was going to take opening some old wounds before Serena and Cole St. Germaine would be able to find happiness.

I believe in writing what I know, and if I know nothing else for sure, I know this: all worthwhile relationships require work, and in order to get on with the future, we often have to confront the demons of our past. But this book isn't all dark. There are some new and interesting people in town, and I'm hoping to be able to write their stories, too. Spirit Creek may be a small town, but it's definitely big on heart. The people in Spirit Creek care about each other–even when they're fighting. I hope you enjoy spending time with them as much as I have.

And remember, I always love to hear from readers. Please visit my Web site at www.LindaStyle.com or write to me at LindaStyle@LindaStyle.com.

May all your happily-ever-after dreams come true,

Linda Style

THE PROMISE HE MADE

Linda Style

TORONTO • NEW YORK • LONDON
AMSTERDAM • PARIS • SYDNEY • HAMBURG
STOCKHOLM • ATHENS • TOKYO • MILAN • MADRID
PRAGUE • WARSAW • BUDAPEST • AUCKLAND

Recycling programs
for this product may
not exist in your area.

ISBN-13: 978-0-373-78326-7

THE PROMISE HE MADE

This edition published by arrangement with Harlequin Books S.A.

www.eHarlequin.com

Printed in U.S.A.

ABOUT THE AUTHOR

Linda Style grew up in Minnesota, where she spent many long, cold winters making up stories in her head. She attended the University of Minnesota, studying behavioral science, married and had four sons. But the dream of writing persisted. After moving to Arizona and earning a degree in journalism from the Walter Cronkite School of Journalism at Arizona State University, she worked in a number of jobs from social services to magazine editor. Since she made her first sale in 1999, her novels have won several contests and awards, including the prestigious Daphne du Maurier Award. When not writing, Linda indulges her passions for travel, photography, hiking in the desert near her home in Gilbert, Arizona, and doing things with her family. Visit Linda's Web site and read an excerpt at www.LindaStyle.com.

Books by Linda Style

HARLEQUIN SUPERROMANCE

1062–SLOW DANCE WITH A COWBOY
1084–THE MAN IN THE PHOTOGRAPH
1155–WHAT MADELINE WANTS
1243–THE WITNESS*
1281–HIS CASE, HER CHILD**
1323–AND JUSTICE FOR ALL**
1361–HUSBAND AND WIFE REUNION**
1443–THE MAN FROM TEXAS
1458–GOING FOR BROKE***
1557–THE MISTAKE SHE MADE

*Women in Blue
**Cold Cases: L.A.
***Texas Hold'Em

To my family
Timothy and Theresa, Todd, Courtney and Connor,
Barry, Jason, Kelly, Kylie, Jack and Luke

ACKNOWLEDGMENT

My deep appreciation to
the Sedona, Arizona, Chamber of Commerce.
Since this is a work of fiction,
I've taken liberties where necessary.
Any mistakes are mine.

PROLOGUE

May 1996

"TRUST ME. I'LL BE back in an hour. I promise." Cole flashed Serena a 100-watt smile, jumped in his El Camino and burned rubber.

She waved and called out, "I love you," then kept waving until the taillights faded into tiny red dots that disappeared into the darkness.

She'd been waiting forever to tell Cole, but every time she started to, she'd lost her nerve. Which was silly, because they'd already made plans to get married and have a family. The family would just happen a little sooner. That's all.

Fingers trembling, she touched the two intertwined silver hearts on the chain Cole had given her as a graduation present. He'd said it meant they would be together forever. Two hearts beating as one. She spun in a circle. For once in her life, things might turn out as she had hoped.

As she stood at the end of the trailer-park driveway, every nerve in her body thrummed. A bright crescent moon had settled over the mountain just above the trees at Oak Creek. Listening to the cicadas in the balmy night air, Serena felt alive with possibility.

This night, their graduation night, would be etched in her heart as the most wonderful, most romantic night ever. And when Cole returned, she'd tell him about the baby.

As Serena walked back to the trailer to get things ready for the celebration she'd planned, a car screeched into the driveway, headlights reflecting off the jagged sheet-metal patches on the tumbledown trailer her parents had parked in the nearly deserted area. The bronze Mercedes pulled up next to Serena, stirring up a cloud of Oak Creek Canyon dust.

Tori. Serena's best friend was always late.

"I'm really, really sorry," Tori said as she got out. "My car has some stupid thing wrong with it and I had to wait until my parents came home to use theirs."

Hugging her, Serena said, "It's okay. You didn't miss much." She shrugged. "You read the draft I wrote. No biggie."

"Stop that!" Tori frowned, then tsked. "You always act like nothing is a big deal. How many kids in your class gave a valedictorian speech?"

Tori didn't wait for an answer. "It *is* a biggie, and I'm bummed I missed it."

One little speech paled in comparison to what she would tell Cole later on. She was so happy about it, she could rocket to the moon on her own power. She couldn't stop smiling, either.

"Where's Cole?" Tori asked.

"He went to the…a party in Sedona one of his friends was having." As she said the words, she could see the disapproval in Tori's eyes. "Just for a while. He promised to be back in an hour."

"An hour." It wasn't a question but a statement.

"Yes. And guess what? I'm going to tell him tonight."

"Really?" Tori shot Serena a doubtful look as she gestured to the two metal lawn chairs near the trailer door. "Really?"

"Yes, really!" Serena said, instantly defensive. "Tonight is the perfect night."

"If he comes back."

"He'll be back just as he said."

Tori sat, then stretched out her legs. Serena knew exactly what her friend was thinking. But Serena was satisfied because he'd promised he would. He'd never made her a promise before. Everything would be fine. She felt it deep inside.

"I just don't want you to be disappointed again," Tori said, then looked away.

Why couldn't Tori just be happy for her? "I won't be." And that was that. She calmed herself, knowing she shouldn't be angry at Tori, because her friend was just watching out for her. As kids they'd made a pact that they'd always be honest with each other. When Tori was about to do something stupid, Serena's job was to call her on it, and vice versa.

"We're going to have our own graduation celebration, and I—" she took a breath "—I'll tell him then."

Tori reached up and smoothed back a strand of Serena's hair. "Hmm."

"Hmm, what?"

"Nothing. Just—" She sat back, hands on her knees. "Just…nothing."

Her friend knew her too well. Serena always waited until she was sure of something before she forged ahead. Living with parents who'd never left the '70s, she'd learned early on not to count on anything until it actually happened.

"Where's your mom?" Tori asked. "And your brother?"

"My mom's taking care of my grandma and Ryan is supposed to be at the school dance." Serena knew Tori wouldn't ask about her dad because he was never there. He spent more time in jail than he did at home. Serena waved a hand. "I didn't tell Cole before because—I...just wanted..."

She really hoped the news wouldn't keep Cole from going to college as they'd planned. Aware of how strongly Cole felt about his father having abandoned his family, she was afraid he'd think he had to get a full-time job to support them. "I just didn't want to mess things up. College is our only way to get out of Spirit Creek and make something of our lives."

"That's not true," Tori said. "You're smart. You can do anything you want."

"You only say that because you've always had everything. Your parents can send you to school and pay for you to stay in a dorm and all that stuff. It's not like that for me or Cole. We have to work our butts off, and even then we don't—" Seeing the hurt in Tori's eyes stopped Serena. "I'm sorry. I only meant—"

"Nope." Tori raised a hand. "You can't be sorry for telling the truth. Geez." She shook her head. "I *don't* know what it's like, so I say dumb things."

They sat side by side in silence for a moment. Finally, Serena said, "You're the best friend ever."

Tori leaned over and hugged Serena again. "So, what's the plan?"

Serena swatted a moth hovering near the

string of Christmas twinkle lights still hanging on the trailer. "Same as before. Now that we've both been accepted to ASU, everything will be fine. I'll just be pregnant while I'm going to college. No big deal." With college degrees behind them, she and Cole would never have to worry about a roof over their heads or where their next meal was coming from. Their child would never go hungry or feel he or she wasn't good enough.

She placed a hand on her stomach, just as she'd done a million times since missing her period four weeks earlier, and wondered when she'd feel the baby move.

"Is that new?" Tori asked, fingering the chain at Serena's neck.

"Uh-huh. It's from Cole."

"Nice!" Tori said as she examined it. "Very nice." Then she glanced at her watch. "You've got plans. I better go."

"You've got to at least have some champagne. I still have that bottle you took from your parents' party."

"I can't. But come over tomorrow morning and tell me what happens." Tori launched herself to her feet, went to her parents' car and slid into the driver's seat.

"I'll call you tomorrow first." Serena stood up. As she watched Tori leave, her heart felt so full she thought it might burst. She closed her eyes and breathed in the scent of cedar and pine from someone's nearby campfire. This *was* the most wonderful night of her life. Even the warm air felt as if it was embracing her. She eyed her watch. Only thirty minutes before Cole would return.

She touched the necklace and sank into the chair to wait.

And wait.

Two hours went by before she got up, as if in a trance, to go inside. As she did, a car turned into the trailer park's long driveway and stopped about ten yards in front of her parents' trailer, its bright lights shining directly into her eyes. A huge wave of relief rolled through her.

Anything could've happened to make Cole late. Late was better than never, she rationalized. She had to be understanding. Too much at stake not to be.

She started walking toward the car, then broke into a jog, holding one hand up against the glare of lights. As she got closer, the lights went out. A second passed before her eyes adjusted. Then she froze.

It wasn't Cole. It was the sheriff. And someone else.

She was used to seeing the sheriff's car—the sheriff had come often enough for her dad. But he was in jail in Phoenix. And the sheriff couldn't be there about anyone else in her family.

Sheriff Masterson didn't get out. He just sat there. She was about to walk over, when a deputy exited from the passenger side and strode toward her.

"Hello, Serena," the man said.

She recognized him. Jason Ramirez had graduated three years ago. He looked serious.

"I'm afraid I have some bad news," he said.

Serena's heart almost stopped. She could barely get out the words. "Cole? Is it Cole?"

"No. He's okay," Ramirez said quickly. "Is your mom home?"

It took a moment for that to register. Cole was okay. He was okay. Tears welled and she released a long breath. Thank God, Cole was okay.

"Is your mom here?" he asked again.

"Oh. No, my mom's…not here. She's taking care of my grandmother." Then it dawned on her that if he wanted to talk to her mother, her twin brother, Ryan, was probably in trouble again.

"Can you get her on the phone? There was a bad accident tonight and I need to talk to her. Your brother was involved."

"My bro—" She shook her head. "He—he's with Celine."

Ramirez moved to stand next to her and

placed a hand on her shoulder. "Serena, I need to talk to your mother."

"Where is he? Where's Ryan?" she demanded. "Is he all right?"

The deputy glanced at the sheriff, who was still in the car. Serena started to walk to him, but Ramirez stopped her with a hand on her shoulder. "Ryan is in the hospital. I guess there isn't any way to do this gently, so I'm just going to say it. Your brother and Cole are both in the hospital and…Celine…" He looked at the squad car again. "Celine didn't make it."

CHAPTER ONE

I'LL BE BACK IN AN HOUR. I promise. Serena Matlock remembered Cole's exact words as she stood at the front window of the Cosmic Bean and watched the silver BMW stop a block down.

It hadn't been an hour. It had been thirteen years. Thirteen years, a baby, a divorce, a college degree and a new business since Cole St. Germaine had said that to her on the night of their high-school graduation. But more than the words she remembered the heartbreak.

She watched Cole get out of his vehicle and climb the steps of the Purple Jeep Touring Company, his once boyish face now that of a man—a man who still carried himself with confidence, even though in high school that confidence had stemmed from a humongous chip on his shoulder.

He'd filled out over the years, and his dusty-blond hair seemed even thicker than the last time she'd seen him—at the jail when she'd told him goodbye. Her throat closed and she swallowed. Cole St. Germaine was back.

She shut her eyes. *Damn you, Cole. Why did you screw everything up? Why did you have to come back?*

Serena swung around to face her friend Natalia, who sat in one of the easy chairs a few feet from the café window. "Does he think everything will be fine? Does he think no one will remember?" An angry knot formed in Serena's stomach.

Business had slowed since the breakfast group had arrived and left, so she went back to the coffee bar to clean the copper espresso machine.

"Maybe he doesn't care what other people think."

"Well, you're probably right about that. He never cared before, so there's no reason to believe he might now."

Serena ground her teeth and polished the copper even harder. "I don't get why my brother is so willing to bend over backward for someone who never gave a rat about him."

"I thought they were friends."

"We were all friends. But when a friend screws you over, he's not a friend anymore."

Natalia shrugged. "Apparently, you're the only one who feels that way."

"Well, friendship won't fix the leg Ryan almost lost. It won't bring his business back from bankruptcy. Some things can't be fixed."

Like the night Cole said he'd return…the night she was going to tell him about the baby and he'd blown her off to party with his friends…and Ginny Gentry.

Like her brother's injuries…and…her and Cole's baby. The baby she'd given up for adoption. Without ever telling Cole she was pregnant.

"Do you know what happened that Ryan had to file for bankruptcy?" Natalia asked.

"Only what he told me, that the business didn't bring in enough money to pay his mortgage and other bills. And if he doesn't get on the ball and start doing something, he'll be in even worse shape."

"Well, if it's any consolation, a lot of people are having that problem right now."

After pausing to get her breath, Serena said, "Yeah. That's true." Yet, Ryan's financial woes weren't burning a hole in Serena's gut. It was the fact that Ryan could simply pick up his friendship with Cole as if nothing had ever happened.

But Natalia wouldn't understand. Though Serena had told her friend almost everything—that Cole had been the love of her life, the father of her child—she couldn't tell Natalia or anyone what it was like to lose a child. To wonder where that child was, if he was happy, healthy…or if there was something she could've done differently. That burden was hers alone.

And it would stay that way.

Natalia sipped her coffee. "Maybe he's just here to visit his mom and won't be here too long."

"Any time is too long for me." What had happened that night had been a defining moment in her life. Cole's reckless behavior had changed everything. Nothing would ever be the same. Not for any of them.

She continued wiping down the sides of the espresso machine, which took up one end of the old soda-fountain counter she'd salvaged from a Flagstaff drugstore that was going out of business. Almost everything in the café—the old ice-cream tables and chairs, the easy chairs, jukebox, the embossed-copper tiles behind the counter, the kitchen equipment—had been salvaged from somewhere.

The bell on the door jingled and she looked up to see Ryan walk in. "Hey, ladies."

"Hey," Serena answered as he walked toward her for a hug. For twins, Ryan looked nothing like Serena. She was fair like their father, whereas Ryan resembled their mother, a dark-eyed brunette who liked to flaunt her gypsy heritage. Ryan's undisciplined nature was similar to their mother's, too, and the exact opposite of Serena's. She liked order, liked to have a plan, liked to know as much as she could whenever she had a decision to make.

"Good news," Ryan said. "I have a way to get the business out of Chapter 11."

"That *is* good news. I wasn't aware anything could do that."

Serena took a deep breath. Every time she saw Ryan and the scar that covered the metal plate in his head, or saw him struggle to do something with his bad leg, she was reminded that Cole had never meant what he'd told her. In fact, he'd out and out lied. But she'd been young and in love and her love had colored everything…even common sense.

"I'm thinking a good advertising campaign will bring in more business. I'll need some help in that area, though, someone who has the expertise."

"And where will you get money for that?" Serena wadded the towel into a ball and chucked it into the dirty-towel bin. She walked over and stood in front of Ryan, feet apart, hands placed on the counter. "I'm tapped out. You know that."

Her brother drew back. "I'm not asking you. I have another idea."

"Geez, Ryan. Even if you could get the money, throwing good money after bad isn't the way to go. It might be better to start figuring out another occupation. Go back to school…get some training."

Ryan threw his hands into the air and headed down the hall toward the bathroom. "I screwed up. I admit it. But I didn't do it on purpose, and I'm going to fix it."

He reached into his shirt pocket and immediately Serena's nerves went on alert. "Ryan?"

He turned, and when she realized he had a cell phone in his hand, she heaved a sigh of relief. No pills.

"What?"

"Um…nothing." She waved him off.

He began walking again. "Just forget it. Okay? Forget I even mentioned it."

Forget it. She could forget a lot of things, but her brother's welfare wasn't one of them. As twins, she and Ryan had rarely been separated. Even during the period she'd spent in Phoenix when she was pregnant, he'd come with her, had dropped out of college. Then they'd enrolled at ASU together.

After the baby, and a brief marriage that never should have been, she'd gotten her act together, and now everything was turning out just the way she wanted. She had great friends, lived in the most beautiful part of the state, her flaky parents were finally settled in Oregon and her café was holding its own.

Up till now, with the exception of Ryan's problems, everything in her life had been going smoothly. And if she had anything to do with it, it would continue that way.

"I'll be leaving now," Natalia piped up.

Oh, God. Serena had forgotten Natalia was there. "Geez, I'm sorry, Natalia. I just get so upset with Ryan—"

"It's okay. I totally understand. I have a flight in a couple of hours, and I should get ready."

Natalia had moved to Spirit Creek five years earlier, not too long after Serena had moved back, and they'd quickly become good friends. As a helicopter pilot in Iraq for four years, Natalia was now using her skills as a search-and-rescue pilot. "Do you want some coffee to go?"

"No, thanks. I've had my fill. I'm outta here."

Serena watched until Natalia got into her red Mustang convertible and sped away. Hearing that Ryan had returned, she pivoted. "You make people uncomfortable when you spout off like that."

"What? You're the one who started it. Besides, it was only Natalia."

"Precisely. Friends deserve respect." Serena

grabbed a dishcloth to clean off the counter. If she said anything else, she'd probably regret it.

"Look at you," Ryan said, sitting on a stool. "You're wound so tight your head's going to snap off. I know it's because Cole is back. Why don't you just chill. A long time has gone by. We're not the same people we were years ago. Cole's not the same."

She stopped and gazed at him, head cocked. "You're probably the only person in this town who believed that."

In a small town like Spirit Creek, everyone knew everyone and everything about them. Loyalties ran deep and memories stretched long. People *didn't* forget. It was one of the things Serena both loved and hated about her hometown. Funny how being away for five years had made her miss even the bad parts. "I noticed the sheriff giving Cole a ticket this morning. I bet *he* hasn't forgotten anything."

"My guess is that the sheriff is just doing his job. Cole has to remember he's not driving in Chicago anymore."

"So, you're defending him now?"

"I'm not defending anyone," Ryan said. "What I'm doing is trying to get a cup of plain black coffee. Not that double-, triple-, super-espresso, mocha-latte-flatte crap I can't even pronounce and that you charge an arm and a leg for."

Serena stifled a laugh. Her brother had a way of talking her down. She sighed, got him a cup and went to sit on the stool next to him. "You're right. I need to chill."

Ryan smiled, dimples showing. Despite the scar running down his temple, he was a good-looking guy. And she loved him dearly, no matter how frustrated he could make her at times. He knew her better than anyone, and sometimes he knew what was going on in her head even before she did. Like the baby. He'd known she was pregnant, even though she'd taken great pains not to tell anyone. The connection between her and her twin was almost eerie.

"You should talk to him," Ryan said out of the blue. "I'm sure he'd like to talk to you."

On that note, she zipped her lips, got up and went to the storage room, where she took out the salt and pepper to fill the containers on each of the tables. But she couldn't keep that fateful night from replaying in her head. Couldn't keep from wondering what she might have done differently. As always, she arrived at the same conclusion. Nothing. Absolutely nothing.

From what Ryan had told her after the accident, he and his girlfriend, Celine, had gotten in the car to talk Cole out of driving. That night Cole had done exactly what he'd told Serena he *wouldn't* do. Instead of making an appearance at his friend's party and then coming back for their own private celebration, he'd stayed, started drinking and ended up with another girl, drunk…and almost dead after missing a turn and crashing into a tree.

For the longest time, she wasn't sure what hurt most. The lies or the betrayal. She was sure that the night was branded in her memory. She'd never forget how Cole had hurt her…how he'd hurt so many people. She'd never forget that he'd ruined *their* future. She couldn't understand why Ryan didn't feel the same. Celine had been his girlfriend. Cole had ruined their future, too.

That Ryan thought she'd *ever* want to talk to Cole again was almost laughable.

She wasn't in the market for more hurt. Not for anyone.

"Okay, if I'm going to get the silent treatment, I'm leaving," Ryan called out. "I've got to make some arrangements for the advertising I told you about."

Serena poked her head out from the storage room. "And how will you manage that?"

Ryan's brow furrowed. "The only way I can." He waited a moment, shifted from one foot to another. "Cole's going to do it. He has advertising experience."

His words hit her like a blow to the stomach with a baseball bat. Suddenly unable to breathe, she reached for the back of a chair to steady herself.

"I don't have any other choice, Serena. I have to do this."

COLE ST. GERMAINE HAD two choices. Confront the problem or ignore it.

He glanced once more down the street to the Cosmic Bean coffee shop, where Serena was carrying boxes from her van into the café.

He couldn't see her face—couldn't see her big brown eyes—but the early-morning sun glinted off her strawberry-blond curls, just as it had when she was seventeen.

He'd spotted her twice in the four weeks he'd been back in Spirit Creek, but she'd always turned the other way—as if she couldn't even bring herself to acknowledge him. And every time, he'd been filled with regret and longing.

She hated him—for good reason.

Cole shook off the feeling. *His* reasons for returning to the small town didn't include mooning over a lost love. He shut the car door and then strode toward the Purple Jeep Touring Company to greet Ryan, Serena's brother.

When Cole's mother had phoned and said she was about to lose her house, Cole had been too shocked to speak. Once he'd found his voice and asked why, she wouldn't say. But Cole knew it had to do with him—and the accident that haunted him even now, thirteen years later. She felt guilty over what her son had done.

Drunk driving. Manslaughter. Jail. That was Cole's legacy in Spirit Creek. And nothing—not his time in jail, not his regret or remorse—could compensate for the sorrow he'd caused so many people. If he hadn't been seventeen at the time, he would've spent longer than a year in jail.

Ryan nodded toward Serena's café. "She'll thaw out sooner or later."

Cole settled one foot on the bottom step of Ryan's store, turned and looked again. "Doesn't matter. I'll be leaving as soon we get this business back in the black."

Ryan frowned, then went inside. Cole followed. Apparently, his old friend didn't like being reminded why Cole was there. Growing up, he and Ryan had been as close as brothers, and Cole's mother had taken Ryan under her wing like a second son. Ryan's own mother had been absent most of the time, and he'd reveled in the love and attention Cole's mom bestowed on him.

"Business should pick up now that the

weather is cooling down," Ryan said as he went around the rustic wood desk and opened the blinds. "Then everything will be fine." He cleared his throat. "And you can go back to your other life."

Ignoring the edge in Ryan's tone, Cole said, "I hope. Filing for Chapter 11 buys time to reorganize the business, but it's time we have to use wisely."

Ryan stopped in place and ran a hand through his hair. "Yeah, I know." He let out a long sigh. "I'm really sorry, Cole. Your mom insisted on helping me, and I never in a million years expected the business to tank."

Cole wanted to say that Ryan could've refused to take her money, refused to let her cosign his loan, but he bit back the words. Pointing this out to Ryan would only put a bigger wedge between them. "Forget it. What's done is done. We've come a long way in a short time."

"Yeah." Ryan glanced away. "The place looks great now, which should help."

Amazing what a little cleanup could do. Cole was sure the elbow grease and the small amount he'd spent to buy paint and furniture was well invested. The touring company's office looked inviting, with its rustic wood floors and Southwest furnishings. And the photographs and posters on the walls, depicting the various tours, were tantalizing. All bespoke adventure of the Old West. Some tours went to the old Indian ruins with petroglyphs and to the Montezuma's Castle cliff dwellings; some to old mines and ghost towns; and some to the vortex-energy sites.

Ryan walked over to a window, and Cole noticed that Ryan's gait was still off because of injuries from the accident. Ryan stared out and said, "I've got to go to Phoenix for the next couple of days, and seeing as how we don't have a whole lot on the books, you probably won't miss me."

"No problem for me," Cole said. "But if business does pick up, we'll have to turn it down with only one of us here."

"There are a few college students in town who could fill in."

"Do they know the tours?"

"No, but they live here. That's good enough."

And that was part of the reason the business had gone under. Good enough *wasn't* good enough.

"Serena uses a couple of them at the café off and on. They're cool."

Serena. Just everyday conversation…every day. He forced himself to focus. "Okay. Just write down their names and numbers."

He liked it that people in Spirit Creek were

willing to help out at a moment's notice. That didn't happen a whole lot in the large cities he'd lived in over the years. On the other hand, he'd never gotten close enough to anyone in those places to find out. Remaining anonymous was easy in a big city.

"So, are you good with that?" Ryan asked. "Me being gone?"

"Do I have a choice?" He laughed, attempting to make light of the situation.

"If you need me, you've got my cell number." Ryan turned to go to the coffee room.

The whole time Cole had been back, Ryan hadn't said a word about Cole's disappearance following his release from jail twelve years earlier, but it felt like the proverbial elephant in the room. The night of the accident, Ryan had told Cole not to be stupid. He'd attempted to convince Cole not to drag race. But, as usual, Cole couldn't pass up a dare. He'd never been able to, not since he was five and some of his classmates had taunted him and jeered him because he wore clothes from Goodwill and his mom cleaned their houses. He'd always had to prove himself and everything else be damned.

But the only thing he'd proved that night was that he was exactly the person everyone thought he was.

Cole touched Ryan's shoulder, and Ryan turned.

"Sorry I didn't stay in contact," Cole said.

Ryan shrugged. "No big deal."

"Yes, it is. I screwed up." He took a huge breath. "I realize saying sorry doesn't fix anything, but I am. I truly am." After Ryan had been released from the hospital, he'd attempted to visit Cole in jail, but Cole had refused. Seeing Ryan only reminded him of what he'd done.

When Cole was released, he'd thought cutting ties would help him forget. But there had been no escape. Not in Chicago, where he'd worked and somehow managed to get a marketing degree, not in New York, Las Vegas, Cleveland or Dallas, where his job had sent him. He couldn't escape himself.

"Okay," Ryan said. "But I screwed up, too." He looked around, shrugged and splayed his hands. "So, let's call it even and go from here."

Cole nodded. "Sure."

"And now I need to make some coffee." Ryan continued to the small storage area that doubled as a break room. "Thanks to Serena I'm addicted to the stuff."

Cole tensed at hearing her name again, picked up one of the brochures from the reception desk and started reading. He had one task in Spirit Creek: resurrecting Ryan's failing business.

Creating the brochure he now held was one of the first things he'd done after he'd arrived, and it had turned out well. Ryan had done nothing to market the business, apparently depending only on word of mouth. Word of mouth was definitely important, but people had to be aware of a product before that could happen.

"Okay, I guess I better get some things together for the tour," Cole said in a loud voice so Ryan could hear him.

Ryan returned, a covered disposable cup in his hands. He checked the time. "First one is at ten. The short Sinagua Ruins tour."

"Yeah, but I have to do some quick research," he said, following Ryan to the door. Cole knew the area, but after so many years away, things had to have changed. Landmarks, new construction. He also didn't know the facts that he should in order to act as a tour guide. He'd been too busy to find out earlier, so some massive research on the Internet was definitely in order.

As Cole stood in the doorway watching Ryan leave, he couldn't help glancing down the street again.

He hadn't been inside the café, but from the looks of the place—a big old Victorian house painted lavender, with white gingerbread trim and, on the street side, a mural of the universe and the red-rock mountains of Sedona where the energy vortexes were rumored to be—Serena seemed to have taken up where her hippie parents had left off. Odd, since she had been so intent on not wanting to be anything like them.

Cole wasn't surprised that Serena owned her own business, but he had been surprised that she was still in Spirit Creek. Neither of them had wanted to stay in the small town. For three months before graduation, they'd spent nearly every day together making plans to leave, to go to ASU in Tempe, get married and have a family. Even back then, he'd wanted that more than anything.

But he'd blown it. One of his biggest regrets. One of many that dogged him every day.

Still watching, Cole saw the sheriff's cruiser pull up to the café, and then someone wearing a uniform got out. From the rotund build, he could tell it was Sheriff Masterson, whose daughter had died in the accident. Cole closed his eyes. As much as he wished he could leave town, he couldn't. He needed to be here. And, he realized, not just to help his mother out.

The time had come for him to face his demons. Face the people whose lives he'd wrecked.

Face Serena.

CHAPTER TWO

"I DON'T WANT TO TALK about it," Cole's mother, Isabella St. Germaine, said. Then she clamped her lips, turned her back on Cole and continued stirring the pot on the stove.

Cole felt his shoulder muscles tighten. Man, his mom was stubborn. Most people her age would want to move to a place that didn't require so much upkeep, like a condo in Prescott…or Phoenix, as he'd suggested. What he'd really like was for his mom to move to Chicago to be near him. But that was out of the question—she hated the cold. Not to mention that he could be out of a job soon and might be moving himself.

Like many businesses affected by the downturn in the economy, Atria Advertising, the company he worked for, was in dire straits, and he didn't know from one week to the next if he'd even have a job. His boss had appeared almost relieved when Cole had asked for time off.

"Fine. But at least think about it," Cole said. "Take a look around here." The sharpness in his tone surprised him. But he was only saying the obvious. He'd never seen the place in such bad shape.

He had to give her credit though. Her stubbornness had gotten them through some rough times. Staunchly independent, Isabella St. Germaine prided herself on being self-sufficient. She'd never have told him about the loan to Ryan and asked for help if everything had gone as she'd expected.

"I have a little headache," his mother said suddenly. "I'm going to leave the stew to simmer and lie down for a while."

Damn. He had to be the most insensitive person in the world. All his mom had ever done was work to make a decent life for him, and even in this instance, she'd acted because of him…because Ryan had been Cole's best friend. "Hey." He touched her arm as she started to walk away, her shoulders slumped. "I'm sorry, Mom. I'm just concerned about you, that's all. I shouldn't be telling anyone what to do." Hell, he'd spent a long time cleaning up his own act, and still had plenty of work to do in that department. "I won't bring it up anymore."

"No need to be sorry," she said on her way to the stairs. "You're a good son."

She always said that, and in her eyes, he probably was, even though he didn't deserve the designation. "Okay. You rest. I'm going out to mow the lawn."

When Cole had first arrived, he couldn't believe how frazzled his mom had looked. Probably the stress from what was happening with Ryan. He wished she'd told him *before* Ryan had filed for Chapter 11, which wasn't quite as bad as Chapter 7. The former, Chapter 11 type of bankruptcy allowed a business to restructure and make an effort to pay the bills. He just hoped that was possible.

After his mom had gone, Cole went into the kitchen for a bottle of water, then outside to get the mower. Within an hour and a half, he'd mowed both the back and front lawns. Though it was early September, he was sweating profusely.

Standing at the edge of the driveway, he wiped his face with the hem of his T-shirt. Why his mom still insisted on having grass, when every other house had desert landscaping, was beyond him.

The large ranch-style home sat on an oversize corner lot one block behind Main Street. Its once-white paint was now peeling and crusty, like yellowed onion skins stuck to the clapboard siding.

Over the years, he'd asked his mom if she needed money to keep up the place, and had even sent money for that purpose. She'd always told him she was doing fine. He knew she had enough money to get by, since the house was paid for and for the past ten years she'd worked at the local farmers' market, until last spring when some developer bought up the property.

That was when he'd suggested she sell the house and move east to be near him. His suggestion had gone over like the proverbial lead balloon. She'd refused and said she'd never move, not until they planted her. His great-grandparents had built the house. It had started as a two-room structure. They'd added on to it over the years, which is why the place now sprawled every which way. The house itself was nothing fancy, but to his mom, its sentimental value was worth far more than any money someone might give her for it.

He'd never viewed the house quite that way, and he'd sent her tickets twice a year to visit him, hoping she'd get used to Chicago and want to move. She'd never warmed to the idea. And she never once mentioned being unable to keep up the house.

He took a swig of water, wiped his brow again and breathed in the scent of freshly mowed grass, an immediate reminder of all the times Serena had come over on Saturday mornings to wait for him while he finished mowing.

He'd been love struck from the second he'd seen the curly-haired redhead in third grade when her family moved into the makeshift trailer park where all the hippies lived.

When he and Serena had gotten together in high school, he couldn't believe someone so sweet and so smart would want to be with a guy like him. He'd been hanging with some of the rowdiest guys in town—her brother being one of them—and ready to drop out of school, when she'd offered to tutor him. That had changed everything.

He started studying harder, got some decent grades and made both his mother and Serena proud.

His gut twisted. He'd wanted to be the kind of father he wished he'd had. Not the kind who could abandon his family without blinking. Not the kind who never cared to know if his son was dead or alive. How could any man reject his own flesh and blood? As far as Cole was concerned, *that* was an unforgivable sin.

He guzzled more water and only noticed the black tricked-out Silverado after he heard a door slam. He glanced up. Eddy Torberg, another of his high-school classmates, walked toward him. "Hey, Cole."

Cole smiled. "Hey, Big Ed. What's up?"

"I'm wondering why you haven't been by the Blue Moon."

Ed, who'd been short and stocky in school, seemed almost as tall as Cole now. Six feet, at least. Apparently Ed and his partner, David MacAllister, now owned the Blue Moon Saloon, a place Cole had so far avoided like the lingerie department in Macy's. He wasn't going to add any fuel to the dying embers of gossip in Spirit Creek and risk their kicking up into pretty good flames. Drinking was what had gotten him into trouble in Spirit Creek, and the locals were not likely to have forgotten it. Especially the sheriff.

"I've been real busy, Ed."

"Okay. As long as you're not holdin' a grudge. This town is too small for people to avoid each other."

Maybe. Clearly Serena was avoiding him, because in the normal course of events in a town the size of a postage stamp, people ran into one another all the time. "I agree, but the two of us may be in the minority."

Ed waited a moment, then said, "It could just as easily have been me in the car that crashed. Kinda woke me up."

"Yeah. Me, too," Cole said. Ed had been in

the other car, but Cole had been the one to lose control…after Ed rammed his car. "Only, my call was too little, too late."

Frowning, Ed tapped one of his tennis shoes against the mower to loosen the grass that had stuck to the shoe when he'd walked over. "Damn. These shoes are new, too. Now they're all stained." He tapped his foot again. "Anyway, I stopped by to tell you I'm the point person for the booths at the fall festival this weekend, and I've had a couple of people cancel on me. I talked to Ryan before he left, but he said he was busy and that I should talk to you."

"Sure. I'll do what I can," Cole said, figuring Ed could do with volunteers to help set up.

"Good. We have to fill up the booths, and it could provide good publicity for the Jeep tours."

Tourists flooded Sedona for the annual jazz festival at the end of September, and afterward many of them migrated the seven miles from Sedona to Spirit Creek. Years ago, the small town had piggybacked on the bigger town's action by creating an art festival that ran at the same time. The Spirit Creek festival also included music, but mostly by local groups. Ed was right. Participating would mean good publicity. The touring company needed business however they could get it. "Yeah. I'm in. Just let me know what I should do."

Ed went to his truck and came back with a packet. "Forms to complete. Just drop them off later at the bar." He started back to his vehicle. "You'll have to write a check for the booth, too."

Cole glanced at the papers. How stupid to think he could stay away from the Blue Moon entirely. Too many events were held there. Charity auctions, weddings, anniversary parties. Not that he'd get invited to any of them. And it wasn't as if he'd go in and hang one on—something that was sounding better and better at the moment. "Okay. Will do."

No sooner had Ed driven away than the sheriff's cruiser pulled in and parked. Cole's pulse raced. Though the sheriff had ticketed his car once since he'd been back, Cole had actually run into him twice. Both times Cole had been at a loss what to say, so he'd just nodded. The acknowledgment hadn't been mutual.

A million times over the past thirteen years, Cole had thought about the words he'd utter to the man whose daughter had died because of him, but right now he couldn't remember any of them. All he remembered was the blood—on his hands, on Celine's face—and the anguish filling her father's eyes as he'd held her, dying, in his arms.

The once-lean sheriff got out of the cruiser, hoisted his belt over his middle and headed toward Cole, determination evident in the set of his square jaw and burly shoulders, which were hiked back with authority. Cole recalled the stance well, and his adrenaline kicked up a notch. But Sheriff Masterson couldn't be here to give him another ticket, not unless it was for running a lawn mower.

The sheriff's hair still looked as though it had been whipped in a blender, except now it was silver instead of black. The sheriff stopped, spread his feet and placed a hand on his gun. "Where's your car?"

"My car?"

"There was a hit-and-run early last night."

Cole's spine went rigid. Did Karl believe he was responsible?

The sheriff fixed Cole with a hardened gaze. "I want to see your vehicle."

Cole thought about telling him his car had been in the garage the whole time he'd been in town. However, he decided there wasn't any point. He simply gestured to the Jeep in the drive.

"We've got a witness who said he saw a car, not a Jeep. A silver BMW. Not many of those in this town except yours."

Cole turned the mower around and pushed it toward the garage, anger knotting his belly. But instead of showing his emotions as he might have years ago, he shrugged, grabbed the garage door and raised it. "You're wasting your time here, Sheriff. But go ahead and look it over."

The sheriff proceeded to do just that, first the driver's side and then the passenger side, where he stopped. The car was several years old, a classic, and Cole had taken great care of it. Karl couldn't find even a scratch.

The sheriff pulled out a pair of glasses from his shirt pocket and leaned down to touch the fender. "You said you haven't driven the car at all?"

"That's right." What the hell was Masterson doing? Trying to trap him into saying something that wasn't true?

Karl squared his shoulders, looked Cole in the eyes. Lips thinning, he said, "I guess you're off the hook." He started to leave.

Cole heaved a sigh of relief. He hadn't done anything, but just talking with the sheriff made his pulse race, his palms sweat. At the same time, he realized if he didn't say something now, he'd regret it. "Karl."

The man turned.

Feeling his throat begin to close, Cole coughed. "I don't know how to say this Karl… because I know there isn't anything I can say that will make any difference."

Silence.

"I'd do anything to take back what happened, but that's not possible, and every day of my life I think about what I did and how many people went through hell because of it." Seeing the pain in the sheriff's eyes, Cole looked away. "God, I'd do anything to change what happened, but I can't and I don't know what else to do."

Shifting his stance, the sheriff crossed his arms and bowed his head. After a long moment, he drew a deep breath and said, "There isn't a day that goes by that I don't think of my daughter, but I made my peace with her death a long time ago."

Cole looked up, not sure he'd heard right. "You—"

"I had to in order to be there for my family."

"If I could just do something…"

Frowning, the sheriff said, "If only that were possible."

Cole raised his head. *Yeah. If only.*

"Well." The sheriff turned. "There is something you can do. I would appreciate it if in your travels you kept an eye out for any shady characters."

"Shady characters?"

The sheriff leveled his gaze at Cole. "I've been contacted by the feds about some drug activity in Spirit Creek. And I've heard some things about Ryan."

Cole jerked back. Was Karl asking Cole to spy on Ryan?

"Just keep it in mind," the sheriff said. "That's all I ask."

The sheriff waited briefly, then banged the fender of Cole's car and lumbered away, shoulders slumped, head down.

SERENA RECOGNIZED the male voice immediately. *Cole.* She turned from the espresso machine in the back of her small booth too quickly, bumped her elbow on the corner of the cup rack and spilled the drink she was making down the front of her red Cosmic Bean T-shirt. She'd barely opened her booth and already she was a mess.

"Need some help?" the older man waiting for his cappuccino asked.

"No, it's okay," she answered, then grabbed a napkin and blotted at the spot. When that didn't help, she plucked one of the gift aprons, bearing the café logo, off the table and hastily put it on. Smiling, she said, "There. I'm good to go."

"I didn't even know this town was here," the man said. "If I hadn't seen the posters in Sedona, I wouldn't have come."

"Well, I'm glad you did. We like to think of

our town as the dessert on the Sedona Jazz Festival's menu." She went to redo the man's order, but she could still hear Cole talking—only now in a lower voice, and she couldn't make out what he was saying. What the heck was he doing there? And so early?

As the man left with his coffee, Serena took a step back, blocking herself so Cole wouldn't spot her if he was nearby. She glanced in the other direction, where people were beginning to filter in. The bulk of the attendees wouldn't arrive until later in the day or toward evening, but there were a few who drove to Spirit Creek first, then traveled to Sedona. Even this early in the morning, excitement hung in the air. Booths of all types lined each side of Main Street, with the Cosmic Bean's booth on one end near the other food booths, close to where a stage had been erected for the festival's entertainment. The previous week, Serena, Natalia and her other best friend, Tori, had all helped to make the fall-inspired decorations for the stage.

At the opposite end of the street was Natalia's booth, where she gave out safety information for hiking the area. In between their booths were others that sold everything from handmade quilts to totem poles carved with chain saws.

The Sedona Jazz Festival lasted the whole

weekend, but the Spirit Creek festival was held only on Saturday. Serena loved to watch the people as they arrived in. When she turned back to her booth, she saw Natalia approaching. She and Natalia had only known each other for five years, but it felt as if they'd known each other a lifetime.

"How's it going?" her friend asked.

"I'm trying to get set up before the crowd swarms, but I've had three customers already."

"Well, I'd kill for caffeine this morning, so let's make it four."

"Double espresso?"

"Perfect. What's with the apron?"

"Advertising." She cursed herself for having gotten so flustered just because Cole St. Germaine was at the festival…somewhere. She retrieved a cup for Natalia's drink and decided to have coffee, too.

When she brought the coffee over, Natalia tipped her head to the left…the direction from which Serena had heard *his* voice. "Talked to him yet?"

"Nope. But I'm not worried about it." She took a quick sip and burned her tongue.

"Did you hear the sheriff was at his place last week about that hit-and-run?"

"No." But Ryan had told her the sheriff was watching Cole. "Does the sheriff have reason to believe he was involved?" From what she'd heard, other than helping her brother, Cole had been scarce around town.

"I don't know. I guess the sheriff is just doing his job. Can't blame him for that." Natalia, wearing black jeans, a black knit top and a silver belt with a Native American design, glanced at Serena, a quizzical look on her face. "Karl wouldn't be unfair because of the accident, would he?"

Serena didn't wish to repeat what Ryan had said, because for all she knew, Ryan was just spouting off. "Who can say. I can see how it could happen." But whether that was the case or not, one thing was certain: she wanted Cole to leave and go back where he'd come from. She had to admit, though, he'd done a lot to help Ryan. Even though Cole and Ryan had once been good friends, she'd wondered why Cole was so willing to help her brother now. What was in it for him? Ryan couldn't pay him. When she'd asked her brother why, all she'd gotten was the "he's a friend" response.

Serena heard laughter. Cole's laughter. Then female voices and more laughter.

She felt an unexpected twinge in her chest. She reached down, snatched up a few vortex maps from a box and slapped them on the table. "I don't know why he's here."

Natalia arched an eyebrow. “Are you kidding? He’s manning the Purple Jeep booth.” She peered down the line of booths. “There’s only one booth between you.”

For a moment, Serena was speechless. “Ryan didn’t sign up for it. He told me that. And…and it wasn’t on the list I saw. If I’d realized, I’d have asked for a different spot.”

Her friend shrugged. “What can I say. He’s there.”

Serena shoved a handful of hair from her face. “Seems to me he’s helping with more than advertising. I’d ask Ryan what’s up, but I haven’t run into him all week. He had to go to Phoenix for something, and he hasn’t answered my messages.”

“I guess you didn’t hear then.”

She leaned against the table, eye to eye with Natalia. “Hear what?”

“That Cole is working at the touring company.”

Serena laughed at the absurdity. All Ryan had said was that Cole was going to help with advertising. Not work there. “That’s almost funny.”

Pulling back, Natalia raised a hand. “Truth. I swear.”

Serena felt her heart sink. When she found her voice, she said, “No, I don’t believe it. Ryan wouldn’t do that. He understands how I feel.”

She shook her head. "No. He just wouldn't." But even as she said the words, she felt an ominous dread. "I—I— Even…even if it's true, I can't figure what good it will do."

Natalia shrugged. "Well, why don't you ask him?"

Her throat closed. "Ask who what?"

"Ryan. Tell him what you heard and ask if it's true."

"Okay." And she would, as soon as Ry returned from wherever he was, or if he even answered his damn phone.

"You could ask Cole. From the looks of the groupies hanging out there, he might be drumming up more business than he wants."

Fighting the urge to look, Serena said, "Is Mac helping out at your booth?"

All three friends, Serena, Tori and Natalia, were participating in the event. This year Natalia had asked David "Mac" MacAllister to help hand out information on CPR and tips for combating emergencies when hiking. The two also planned to give CPR demonstrations twice a day. Tori had a booth to display her paintings, and Tori's fiancé, Linc, was assisting her.

"He is right now," Natalia said. "But he can't stay all day. He was talking with Cole earlier. They seem to have hit it off."

"Oh?" Serena said, interested, but trying not

to appear so. Trained as a Navy SEAL, Mac had been discharged after being injured in Iraq. On return to the States he'd studied physical therapy and boned up on the skills he'd learned as a med tech on the battlefield. Now he flew with Natalia on search-and-rescue missions as her EMT—and he was Ed's partner at the Blue Moon.

"Did I tell you Mac's mother is here, too?"

"No, you didn't," Serena said absently. Her brother hadn't been honest…or at least not forthcoming about Cole actually working there. If he had been, she would have been prepared.

"Damn, I wish Ryan had said something."

Her friend's eyebrows arched.

"Not that it matters," Serena added. "That's all in the past. We were kids, and I put Cole out of my mind a long time ago."

"Hi, there, ladies," a woman's voice trilled.

Natalia snorted.

Both Serena and Natalia smiled and waved at Martha and Maxine, who were walking by. The two fiftyish women ran a small flower shop in Sedona and had lived in Spirit Creek for years.

"Maybe they're kindred spirits," Serena said, returning to what Natalia had said.

"Martha and Maxine?"

"No, Mac and Cole."

Natalia appeared puzzled. "Why do you say that?"

"Because of what you said earlier about Mac being such a loner, and because I know Cole doesn't have many friends in Sprit Creek, either."

Her friend laughed. "Kinda like you and me when we met."

"I wasn't thinking that, but yeah, I guess it is." She didn't like thinking about it. At least, the outcast part. She and Cole had both felt it. Had formed a bond because of it.

Living in the trailer park on the outskirts of Spirit Creek with hippie parents, Serena had grown up enduring the sting of disapproval. To feel accepted in the community had taken her nearly two years after she'd returned and opened the café. And she wasn't even sure she'd made the grade yet with some of the old guard.

"I can't imagine what it's like for him to be back here," Serena said. "People might not mention the accident, but I guarantee you no one has forgotten. It has to be terribly awkward."

"You always think about stuff like that. You should've been a social worker."

Serena scoffed. "Like I need more dysfunction in my life? I have my family for that. Besides, fixing people isn't my strong suit." Not if her brother was any indication.

At the other end of the street, where the stage had been erected, one of the local jazz groups started tuning up. The discordant sounds of guitar strings, a fiddle, piano scales and the bleat of a saxophone reminded Serena of the times she and Cole had sat under the stars, listening to music with nothing more pressing than being with each other. Now, as back then, the pungent scent of pine hung like dusky perfume in the crisp autumn air, reminding her all too quickly of another long-ago night in the backseat of Cole's old Chevy.

"Ryan will be fine, Serena. You've got to stop taking his screwups as a personal failure."

But it *was* personal. And there was nothing she could do about that. "He's my brother. I need to be there for him…for support, if nothing else."

"They say people have to hit rock bottom before they'll decide to do something. Maybe *not* helping would be the best thing in the long run."

Though Natalia hadn't said the words, Serena knew what she meant. "Ryan isn't a druggie."

Natalia looked up at Serena from under her eyebrows. "Okay. What is he?"

"He's—he has…some issues. And he has to take pills for the pain." She swallowed her sudden anger. But Natalia didn't make her angry. The increasing frustration over her inability to help Ryan did. "He has no one but me. That's all." She hauled in some air.

"You're doing it again," Natalia said as she tucked a strand of coal-dark hair behind one ear.

Both Natalia and Tori thought Serena was overprotective of her brother, that she made excuses for him. They thought he needed an intervention. Serena wasn't wearing rose-colored glasses where Ryan and his problems were concerned. Her friends just didn't know the whole story. "I realize I am. But that's just the way it is." She'd made a promise long ago, and she'd never go back on it.

"Okay. I'll butt out and mind my own business."

Serena waved and smiled at Mayor Carlson as he went by. "Lookin' good, Serena," he said, and flashed her a thumbs-up.

"I swear," Natalia said. "That old lecher would be on you in a nanosecond if you gave him the slightest encouragement."

The comment made Serena cringe. "Ew. That's disgusting."

"Natalia, can you come over here for a moment?" a woman requested.

Serena looked over, but didn't recognize the chubby older woman nearby.

Natalia leaned in and whispered, "That's Mac's mother, who's going to be here for two weeks. She's decided Mac and I should be dating."

"Not a bad idea," Serena said.

Natalia rolled her eyes at Serena, then raised her disposable cup. "Thank you very much for advice I don't require."

Serena grinned. "Ditto."

They both laughed then. Watching her friend walk away, Serena thought about Mac and Natalia hooking up. If that happened, she'd be the only one of the three friends who was…unattached.

She started to get out some more cups, then heard raised voices, one—a woman's—louder than the other. "No, let me go."

Everyone nearby turned toward Cole's booth, where Ellen Fletcher, one of their former classmates, stood, eyes wide, lower lip quivering. Her husband, Dan, stood next to her, yanking her arm. "El-len," he said menacingly through gritted teeth. "Dammit. I *said,* let's go."

Serena saw the man dig his fingers into his wife's arm…saw the fear in Ellen's eyes. Everyone knew about Dan Fletcher's bad temper and that he'd been thrown into jail more than once because of it. Still, his wife always took him back. Probably because she was scared to death not to.

When Dan yanked his wife again and then shoved her forward, Serena bolted from her booth, marched directly up to Ellen and put an arm around her. Smiling, she said, "Ellen, I haven't talked to you in ages. Come on over to my booth. I'll get you some coffee and we can chat a little." She eyed Dan. "You don't mind, do you, Dan?"

If looks could kill… But Serena counted on the fact that he wouldn't do anything where anyone might see him. Cowards were like that. "C'mon, Ellen," she said, then nudged her former classmate toward the booth.

They hadn't walked two feet, when Dan said loudly, "Ellen."

The woman waited a second and then faced Serena. "Thank you," she said. "But I really can't. I have to go."

"Hey, Dan," a male voice called out, and within seconds, Cole was standing next to Dan, pounding him on the shoulder like a long-lost brother. "How are you, man? It's been a really long time."

Serena seized the opportunity and nudged Ellen again, and this time Ellen went along toward Serena's booth.

As they were walking, Serena noticed three cheerleader types standing by Cole's table, gawking and whispering behind their hands. And she heard Cole speaking to Dan and heaved a sigh of relief. Then again, Dan had probably been like that when he'd hung around with Cole. The thought occurred to her that maybe Cole had stepped in for that very reason. He'd always been protective. Of his grandmother, his mother, his friends. Her.

At the booth, Ellen's fearful expression was telling, but she said, "It's not what you think, Serena."

Serena went behind the table and prepared the woman a cappuccino. "It's not like what?"

Averting her gaze, Ellen said, "I know what you think, what everyone thinks. But everyone is wrong. Dan is good to me."

Denial. Typical. Serena knew firsthand. "You can tell yourself whatever you want," Serena said. "But the problem doesn't affect just you. It affects your children…and if you let it continue, it will affect them for the rest of their lives."

Ellen brought her cup to her mouth with both hands and Serena spotted bruises on her wrists.

"Think about it. You can get help. I'll help you. There are others who can help you." *Like the sheriff.* As she said the words, Serena realized Ellen had tuned her out, her gaze now on her husband.

"I have to go. Thank you for the coffee, Serena. It was really nice." Then Ellen got up and walked over to Dan. He looked at Serena and grinned, as if triumphant. Then he gave her a two-finger salute, wrapped his arm tightly around Ellen's waist and led her off.

In his place, Serena found herself gazing into Cole's blue, blue eyes. Her breath caught, her heart raced and she needed everything she had in her to pull her eyes from his.

That was when she knew she'd been lying to herself. She hadn't put the past behind her at all.

CHAPTER THREE

COLE GRITTED HIS TEETH and steeled his resolve. But he still felt as though a roll of barbed wire was twisting in his gut.

He knew what Dan Fletcher was capable of and had immediately felt protective of Ellen, who had been the only kid in the school to come to Cole's aid when some of her friends were picking on him. Ellen and Celine were first cousins, and they'd been as close as sisters. He sighed. One more person whose life had been affected by his reckless actions.

If he'd only stopped to think…

Swamped by guilt, he reached down to get a poster to tack onto the canvas behind him. Because of that one horrible night, that one idiotic, teenage chip-on-his-shoulder decision, he'd lost everything. To even think of his own losses was unconscionable, but sometimes he couldn't help it.

During the year he'd spent in jail, and afterward while living in Illinois, Nevada and California, wherever he'd been with his job, he'd done a lot of soul-searching. He'd tried to become a better person, donating both time and money to charities and causes to help disadvantaged teens. Once, he'd been involved with MADD, Mothers Against Drunk Driving, and through them, had talked to students about how one decision made under the influence of alcohol could ruin so many lives.

But not until he'd come home to help his mom had he realized how much he needed to face the people he'd hurt—and in some way to make it up to them.

As if he ever could.

Karl and Marley Masterson had lost their only child. Celine had been one of Serena's childhood friends and Ryan's girlfriend. She'd had a bright future. But because of him, Celine was dead and Serena's brother had been through years of pain and suffering. For all intents and purposes, Cole's mother had lost her son, too. And the list just went on and on.

And to almost everyone, the year Cole had spent in jail hadn't been long enough.

Today, for just a moment, when Serena's eyes caught his, he'd felt as if she'd looked into his soul and hated what she'd seen. He'd wanted to turn away, but he couldn't have dragged his gaze from her if someone had been shooting at him.

Thankfully, she'd averted her eyes. But his heart still thumped painfully against his ribs because she had. He knew what people thought of him, but the contempt hurt worse coming from Serena.

"No one wants you here, Germaine," someone suddenly said from somewhere on his left. He turned and saw Dan Fletcher walking toward him sans wife. Dan's military-short hair had grayed a little over the years, but the hard dark eyes were still the same. "Why don't you just leave now and be done with it."

Blood rushed hot through Cole's veins. His first instinct was to punch the guy, but he held back. Instead, he pulled together his reserves, smiled and said evenly, "I like it here." He crossed his arms and spread his feet. "I like it a lot. What I don't like are guys who beat up on women because it makes them feel more powerful, when, in fact, they're just too chicken to take on someone who's equal."

Dan stood there immobile for a moment, his expression blank, as if he hadn't realized what Cole had said. Then his face turned beet red. Veins bulged in his neck. Sputtering, he raised a fist. Cole squared his shoulders. Dan snarled, then shoved a finger in Cole's face. "Watch your back, Germaine. Don't sleep too deep at night."

Standing his ground, Cole said simply, "Duly noted."

Rage still in his eyes, Dan whirled, as if looking for someone else to punch, then faced Cole again. After he sputtered some more, he growled through his teeth and stomped off.

Cole plastered on a smile and started to greet the half-dozen gawking tourists who seemed to be waiting to see what else might happen, as if they were viewing some kind of reality show.

When one of the bands onstage at the end of the street began to play, Cole heaved a sigh of relief. Music always helped him get his mind on other things. Things that didn't relate to how much some people might want him gone. Things that didn't relate to Serena and how much he wanted to talk to her. Touch her. Kiss her. A fantasy that died.

No, he didn't want to think about any of that, and yet, he couldn't think of anything else.

THE REST OF SERENA'S DAY passed without incident. She had been so busy she'd had to flag down Peter, one of the high-school students who worked at the café once in a while, to help her ring up the sales. Ryan assisted her sometimes, but lately he'd disappeared whenever she needed him. But between her and Peter, they'd managed, and she'd loved watching all the people file by. A couple of guys wearing shirts with the name of a rock band came up and asked about Ryan. She didn't know how Ryan knew them, but figured they were in town for the festival or might even be musicians. Ryan had played the guitar in high school and once had visions of forming his own band, so maybe that was how they'd met, because he still liked to hang with the local musicians.

"How long do you want me to stay?" Peter asked when the number of customers started to slow.

It was 6:00 p.m. and getting dark. Serena didn't stay open late, as many of the booths did, because coffee drinks didn't sell well in the evenings; beer was the preferred beverage. "We're over the rush, so go ahead and leave," she said. "Will you be at the festival for a couple of hours, just in case?"

"Yeah, I'll be hanging out by the music." Serena gave Peter his money and told him she'd call him on his cell if she needed him again.

An hour later, as she was beginning to close up, Tori appeared.

"Where are the pups?" Serena inquired. She'd spent a lot of time babysitting Tori's golden retrievers, Bruno and Cleo, before her friend had met the love of her life, Lincoln Crusoe, and he'd moved in with her. "I haven't seen them in forever."

"Linc dropped them off at Animal Farm before he drove over here. I want them to get used to the place so when we go to Paris later this month, they'll be fine."

"Paris?"

"Yeah. Didn't I tell you?"

Serena's mouth dropped open, but she quickly caught herself. "That's…wonderful. When did all this happen?" It used to be that when something important occurred in her friend's life, Serena was the first to know. But since Tori had fallen in love, all that had changed.

"We only made the decision a couple of days ago. Linc has decided to go to law school and finish the degree he'd started years ago, so we figured it would be wise to take a trip now, before he gets too busy studying."

"Oh." That made sense. "So, why are you leaving the dogs with Travis? You always leave them with me."

Tori laughed. "One, your mother is coming for a visit and two, we'll be gone too long for you to be tied down with someone else's animals. But it would be great if you wanted to take them out once or twice so they don't feel totally abandoned."

"I doubt any animal feels that way with Travis."

"True."

"Probably a good idea they'll be at Travis's, since my mom is so unpredictable. I forgot she was visiting." She felt a stab in her gut at the prospect. She laughed. "Or more like I blocked her trip out."

Serena and Tori both laughed. "You'll have a great time," Tori said.

"Maybe. But if she's true to form, something will ruin it." Serena smiled, then rushed to say, "But that's not important. Your trip really sounds wonderful." She picked up a towel from the table and refolded it. Then she grinned. "So, is this a prewedding honeymoon? Or…an elopement maybe?"

Tori grinned, her wide smile like sunshine beaming happiness in all directions. Serena couldn't be happier for Tori, but at the same time, she felt a little sad…almost as if she'd lost a friend. Or maybe she felt that way because she was reminded that she might never find her own soul mate.

"No way!" Tori hugged Serena. "I'd never get married without you and Natalia at my side."

Serena hugged her back. "Never say never."

Glancing toward Cole's booth, Tori said, "You're right. You don't know what might happen."

Serena let out an exasperated breath and avoided looking, herself. “No. If there’s one thing I can say *never* about, that’s it.”

“So, you’re just going to ignore that he’s here? People do change, you realize.”

“What?” Serena pulled back in shock. “Excuse me, but that is a 180-degree switch from everything you’ve ever said about him.”

Tori’s mouth quirked up. “I know. But that was thirteen years ago. Since then, I’ve learned some things about judging other people. Especially when I don’t have the facts.”

Tori was talking about Linc. She and he had overcome some of the most horrific obstacles to be together. But there wasn’t anything even remotely similar in her situation and Serena’s. “Well, in my case, I have the facts, and nothing can change them.” She turned away and quickly scanned the aisle again, for nothing in particular.

“I spotted Ryan earlier with a couple of guys I’ve never seen,” Tori said. “I went to the store around one o’clock and they were hanging out in back of the Blue Moon.”

“Really? I wasn’t aware he was back.”

Her friend’s eyebrows rose and she gave Serena one of those I-told-you-so looks. Then Tori said, “If you need help with anything, give me a shout. Linc and I are available.”

Recently, both Tori and Natalia had told Serena she should get her brother into rehab. But Serena knew exactly what that would accomplish. An intervention would only make Ryan hate her. "I'll be fine, but thanks anyway," she said. "If Ryan's back, he can help, and Peter also said he'd help again if I needed him." She smiled. "So, I'm covered."

Before Tori could say anything more, Serena reached for the bag with the coffee Tori had ordered earlier and handed it to her. "Let's get together before you leave for Paris. Okay?" She hugged her friend.

"Okay." Tori smiled. "I know when to go. I'll be in touch."

After her friend melted into the crowd, Serena looked over at Cole's booth. Several people were lined up, reviewing the items on his table. Tori was right about some things. Serena had to adjust. They were adults, who could coexist in the same town without bringing up the past. The first chance she had, she'd tell Cole exactly that.

After another hour passed and still no Ryan, Serena finally gave in, called Peter's cell number and asked him to help load things into her van when she was finished packing up. Then she started chucking all her unsold goods into boxes. For a long time, she'd tried not to depend on Ryan to do anything, because the disappointment she felt when he reneged on a promise was always worse. But since he needed extra money and had pleaded with her, she'd relented. Only this time, she'd stipulated that he had to help her today. Stupidly, she'd thought he might actually do it. Then he'd left town without a word. Maybe Tori was wrong about having seen Ryan. It could easily have been someone else.

Most of the booths at the festival remained open until ten or eleven and the bands kept playing until midnight or later, depending on the crowds. In the past, Serena always packed up her things, then returned and enjoyed the evening festivities with friends. Most of the time they just sat on the grass, listening to music, but occasionally, she could get one or two of the guys to dance. Travis Gentry or Quint, who used to work as a handyman around town and had recently become a contractor; or even Brody Romano, one of her former classmates. Brody wasn't a very good dancer, but she gave him kudos for trying.

Cole had been a good dancer, she remembered. Or maybe she'd been so in love she'd just imagined he was. Mostly, they'd stood in one spot, moving ever so slightly to some slow beat, her arms over his shoulders, his encircling her waist, her head nestled into his neck. The memory was so vivid she could almost smell his scent. Feel his hands low on her back, pulling her closer and closer.

The bang of a drum made her glance up from the box she was packing. Onstage, Roger Feldman, from a local band called The Penguins, was beginning his drum solo. It was something he did every year, and it signaled the end of the festival's casual ambience of the day and the start of party time for the night. With that one drum solo, anticipation electrified the air around her, as though something important was about to happen, and the anticipation kept building and building. Tonight, for Serena, the feeling was even more intense. As evening descended, so did the locals. They knew the better jazz groups would soon play. Tourists and locals alike made their way along the line of booths like salmon swimming upstream. Families, seniors, old hippie types like her parents, students, bikers…you name it, they were all there. Somewhere around nine o'clock, the grassy areas next to the bandstand would fill with people, and the dancing would begin on the wooden square in front of the stage.

After packing some T-shirts, she remembered Travis having said he wanted one for his fiancée, so she kept out a size small. Travis

Gentry, the town vet, was thoughtful that way, and she really liked him. He could be fun, and he was always nice to her, always treated her with respect. Why couldn't she find someone like that who also made her feel the way she had when she was with— Oh, man. She stopped right there.

It wasn't as if she hadn't given anyone else a shot. She had. Brody Romano, for one; they'd dated a few times. Her ex-husband, for another. Brett Hamilton had been a high-school classmate, as well. She'd met him again at ASU, where they'd both attended college. That was probably the most lonely and unstable time in her life, especially when Ryan dropped out and moved in with some girl. She so regretted what she'd put Brett through, even if it was only for three months. Knowing that she'd just given up her newborn child for adoption, he'd married her. In the three months their marriage had lasted, she'd run through the litany of Brett's positives more times than she could count and always ended with "He was a wonderful person, *but*…"

In the end, she realized that for him to be married to someone who wasn't in love with him wasn't fair. She sighed. Maybe her friends were right. Maybe she did have a commitment problem. No matter who she went out with, there was always something that didn't jell. Nice guy, *but…*

Was it wrong to want to feel that special spark in a relationship? Was that shallow? No sooner had she thought it than she heard a male voice. She looked up.

"Hey, there, pretty lady," Brody Romano said, his smile a mile wide. "Do you need some help?"

"Nope, I've got everything under control. But thanks anyway. You're too nice."

"I am," he agreed. "But only to pretty women I want to date."

She cast him a sidelong glance.

He raised a hand. "Okay, I know. But you can't blame a guy for trying."

"No. And I truly hope you find the woman of your dreams one of these days."

"Thanks." He frowned. "I think." He rubbed a hand across his chin. Brody was dark and ruggedly handsome, a true gentleman cowboy who managed his father's dude ranch just outside of town. "Well, at least save me a dance later. Okay?"

She smiled as Brody turned to leave. "Sure thing…love to dance." *Loved to dance with Cole.* She resisted the urge to look in his direction. The mere thought of his body molded to hers, moving slowly to soft music, thighs rubbing thighs, made her sweat. They'd been well suited. Very well suited.

Thank heaven her phone rang. She turned away and glanced at the ID. Ryan. Finally. "Hey, Ryan. Where the hell are you?"

"I'm at home. I just got back and I'll be there in a bit to help. All right?"

Ryan lived in a tiny apartment complex outside of town that used to be a motel. His apartment wasn't fancy, but it was all he could afford. She'd encouraged him to put some of the insurance money from the accident into a fund to keep him afloat, but he'd gone through it fast.

"Okay," she said, pleased that he was actually going to do what he'd promised for once. And she was even happier that she didn't have to deal with anything else right now. She wanted to meet her friends and have a night of fun. That was it. She needed more fun in her life.

She went on with the packing. By the time she was halfway through, Ryan still wasn't there. She called Peter, and the two of them finished up. She took an armful to load into the van while Peter packed up the small trucking cart she used for the bigger things. On her way back, she was surprised to see Dan Fletcher at the booth next to Cole's, his hands clenched into fists. Cole was standing in front of his booth, doing something, but his back was to her. She saw Dan turn, his eyes narrowed.

Her heartbeat quickened.

In one sudden step, Dan was at Cole's side. As Cole pivoted, Dan shoved him. Cole staggered; then, righting himself, he brushed off the front of his shirt and squared his shoulders. Oh, God. Cole had never accepted any guff from anyone, and she fully expected him to respond swinging. But he didn't. He just stood there.

Dan shoved Cole again, only this time harder, slamming Cole back against the table. Serena gasped. Dan hovered over Cole, his face contorted with rage. Cole drew his arm back, and just as he swung, the table collapsed and the two men crashed to the ground with it.

Serena quickly tried to spot Ellen. If Dan hadn't taken out his temper on his wife already, he surely would now. But she didn't notice Ellen anywhere. Serena rushed over, unsure what she could do, but it seemed she should do something.

As Dan rose, he glimpsed her and pointed. "You. This is your fault."

Serena glanced around, not realizing he was talking to her.

"She's gone, and it's your fault. Both of you."

Cole was on his feet and instantly positioned himself between Serena and Dan. "You better take a walk and cool down," he said to Dan.

"Maybe I should haul y'all in," another voice boomed from somewhere nearby.

They looked to the left and saw Sheriff Masterson walking over.

Dan bolted, gone in a flash. Serena smoothed her hair and glanced at Cole, but she wasn't about to gaze into his eyes. Then she felt his hand on hers. She couldn't think…couldn't move. Her heart thudded in her ears like thunder. She forced herself to pull away, and then she bolted, too.

Back to her booth. Back to safety.

CHAPTER FOUR

ON HER FINAL TRIP to the van, someone called out, "Serena."

A female voice. Serena stopped, looked up. Natalia, still at her booth, raised her hands, palms up, as if to ask what was going on. Serena shrugged. As she started for the parking lot again, she felt a hand on her shoulder. She swung around.

"Hey, sis. I made it."

She could barely contain the annoyance she felt. "For what? I'm all done now." She glanced around to see if anyone was in earshot just in case Ryan went off on her as he could sometimes. Mrs. Gentry, the town matriarch, and a few of her cohorts were standing nearby, wearing their ever-ready judgmental faces.

Her brother tossed her a look of indignation. "Well, I could've not come at all."

"Right. You could've. So why did you?"

"Well, pardon me for not meeting your schedule for my life."

She stared at him, incredulous that he could in any way, shape or form make this statement about her. Keeping her voice low, she said, "Ryan, you took my money and promised you'd be here to help me as a way to earn it. You knew what time you had to be here, and now you want to make this about me? I don't think so."

Ryan huffed. "You don't get it, do you? I'm not a kid you have to watch over anymore. Tell me where to be and when."

If only that were true. Serena took a deep breath and ran a hand through her hair. "God, this is ridiculous. Are you forgetting—" She glanced to where Mrs. Gentry stood, then back to Ryan, her expression beseeching him to keep his voice down. That was when she saw his eyes were bloodshot, his pupils dilated.

"Dammit, Ry," she said under her breath. "Look at you. Maybe I should've just let you do whatever and be done with it. Then I could start visiting you in jail the way we did Dad all those years."

He stood there staring at her for a moment, then waved a hand and tromped off, muttering, "I'm not taking this crap any longer. I'm outta here."

As he mumbled the words, Tori and Linc walked up with a load of Tori's paintings, heading to the parking lot, as well. "Hey, are you okay?" Tori asked.

"I'm fine. Same old, same old," she said, debating whether to go after Ryan.

Intuiting what Serena was thinking and aware what had happened in the past, Tori said, "Let him go. He'll cool off and be fine."

She sighed. "I wish I could be that certain. His behavior is so…different lately."

"Maybe it's because of him." Tori tipped her head in Cole's direction.

"Cole? He's helping Ryan. Ryan should be grateful, not having problems."

Linc raised an eyebrow. "'Pride cometh before the fall,'" he said.

If Linc only knew. Pride hadn't stopped Ryan from anything else; she couldn't imagine it would now. Her brother loved Cole, much to her chagrin. But Tori's fiancé hadn't been around all that long and wasn't well acquainted with her brother. "I'll keep that in mind," she said. "You could be right."

"We're going to take this stuff home," Tori said. "But we'll be back later. You can buy me a beer." She smiled wide as only Tori could. Beautiful, talented beyond compare, with personality to spare, and really smart, Tori was everything Serena wished she could be.

"You're on," Serena said. A small sense of relief rippled through her—until she looked up and saw the sheriff standing with Mrs. Gentry and pointing toward Cole's booth. The skin on her nape prickled. "I'll get a group together," she said absently as Tori and Linc left.

She quickly drew her gaze away. Why she felt any sympathy for Cole was beyond her. The last thing he would ever want or need was sympathy.

After she finished up, Serena ambled over to the food section and decided not to wait for any of her friends to order. "Number four, Joe." A basket of baby-back riblets and fries.

"You want a beer, too?" inquired Joe, whose voice was as full-bodied as the rest of him.

"Sounds great!" The sad truth was, she'd need a lot more than one to have the fun she was determined to have tonight.

COLE STROKED HIS CHIN AND watched Ryan stalk off in one direction while Serena went in another. Dan's swipe at him hadn't connected, and then he'd been stunned by Serena's sudden appearance. In fact, he'd been so stunned he'd been unable to get a word out. And then she was gone.

He turned to see if the table was damaged. One of the legs had folded under his weight, but apparently no harm had been done. He snapped the leg back in place and began picking up the Native American artifacts and brochures that he'd placed on his table to interest those who passed by. As he reached down for the arrowheads that had spilled from the box, he glimpsed the toe of a snakeskin cowboy boot.

"What's goin' on, Cole?"

He recognized Ed Torberg's voice and rose to face him. "Not much. I leaned on the table and it collapsed, that's all."

"That's not what I heard." Ed frowned. "People around here talk. You know that."

Cole steeled his resolve. "I do." So what was the big deal to Ed, anyway?

"Someone said you started a fight with Dan Fletcher." Ed glanced at the table leg, crossed his arms and shifted from one foot to another. Under his breath, he said, "I don't know how I got this damn job in the first place, but now that I have it, I gotta make sure nothing goes wrong."

Anger coiled in Cole's belly. He clenched his hands, an attempt to quell the volcanic action ready to erupt from within. He forced a smile. "Everything's just fine with me, Ed." As far as Cole was concerned, it was. "But someone might want to keep on eye on Ellen Fletcher."

Ed frowned and shook his head, as if that

suggestion was something he didn't want to hear. "I stay out of other people's business," he said, then his voice switched low, his tone now sympathetic. "Just so you know, I had a hard time getting your application approved, so I don't want to be proven wrong about doing it."

Cole straightened. "I appreciate it, Ed. I really do." He could tell it wouldn't do any good to explain he hadn't said or done anything to start the skirmish. Apparently, no one wanted to acknowledge spousal abuse.

At that moment, Travis Gentry's grandmother, who'd been a widow since Cole was old enough to remember, walked by, eyeing him as she had when he was a kid. She owned the bank and a hell of a lot of property in Spirit Creek, and she ruled the huge Gentry family, her last will and testament clenched in her fist.

What Amelia Gentry said mattered in Spirit Creek, and many of the old-timers looked to her for direction on just about everything that happened in the small town. Cole was *real* familiar with the matriarch. For years his mother had cleaned the Gentry place on the hill just on the outskirts of town. Cole and Travis had played together…until the elder Mrs. Gentry had put a stop to it.

He and Ed watched the woman walk away, then Ed said, "Old biddy." He turned to Cole.

"For what it's worth, it took a long while for people to see that I'd changed and that I'm not the hell-raiser I was in high school," he said. "Give it some time."

"Thanks." Cole clapped him on the shoulder. "That's good to know." Except that he didn't have time. Even if he wanted to, he couldn't stay in Spirit Creek forever.

Ed smiled, and Cole noticed that the slight overbite many of the kids had made fun of back in the day had been fixed.

"So," Ed said, "a bunch of us are going to have a stag party for Travis next Friday. He's getting married in a couple of weeks."

"Really?"

"Didn't Ryan tell you?"

Cole shook his head. Ryan hadn't said a word. Neither had his mother. "Nope. But Ryan's been gone a lot, so we haven't had much chance to talk. Doesn't matter, because I've got a full schedule, anyway." And from the scorn in Mrs. Gentry's eyes, Cole doubted a renewed friendship between Travis and him would come anytime soon, much less be received with open arms.

As Ed started to go, he said, "Hey, stop by the bar when you can. There're always a few of the guys hanging out or playing pool. Maybe you'll want to get in on the tournament."

Cole had no doubts that going to the bar

would be the worst thing for him to do. But those who thought the poorest of him thought it anyway, so going didn't really matter. "Sure. Maybe I will."

The music that had been playing in the background, mostly upbeat stuff, became a little softer and switched to a slow yet jazzy version of Seal's "Kiss from a Rose." The song brought back more memories than he wanted. He turned to see what band was playing…and spotted Serena, who was dancing with one of their former classmates, Brody Romano. Cole's gut clenched. No, he was wrong about going to the bar. There was something else that would be the worst thing he could possibly do.

And, God help him, he just might do it.

THOUGH SERENA WAS DANCING with Brody, she was still shaking off the sensation of Cole's warm touch. She and Cole had been eye to eye, skin against skin…and before she knew it, her old longings and desires had come rushing back. *Silly. Really silly.* She focused on Brody, trying to put her mind on her dance partner, where it should be.

"So, how about it?" Brody pulled back to look at her.

"I…I'm sorry. What did you say?"

He frowned, his eyes darting as if he wanted to see what might've taken her attention away from him. "I asked if you'd like to go to a movie with me tomorrow. Not as a date, though. Just as a friend."

"I—I don't know. I'll…have to check my schedule," she said, sounding far too business-like. But those were the only words that popped to mind. Being friends with someone she'd dated was fine if it could really be that way. Only, in her experience it never could. "If I can't go, I bet there are any number of women who'd want to go with you."

Abruptly, his hold tightened. "I don't care to go with any number of women, Serena. I want to go with you."

Serena instantly pulled away. She'd never seen Brody so uptight. And she didn't like it.

He must've sensed her discomfort, because he said, "I, uh…I don't have any other friends quite like you."

She coughed to stop him from saying anything more. "I'll have to check and let you know. And right now, I really, really need to find the ladies' room." She pivoted and headed toward the park facilities, leaving him in the middle of the dance floor.

"I'll wait over there," he said, pointing to the first-aid booth, where Natalia was giving the last CPR demo of the festival. He smiled. "So we can finish our dance."

She shook her head. "No. It's been a long day. I'm kinda tired."

He frowned. "It's him, isn't it? It's Cole. You've still got a thing for him, don't you?"

She ignored his questions and kept going, and then she stayed in the bathroom for as long as she could. She didn't want to sit with Brody any more tonight. She didn't want to dance with him, either. And if he didn't understand, she'd make it perfectly clear.

She washed her hands a second time, then slowly dried them with a paper towel. When she had first moved back to town and bought the old Victorian house that eventually became the Cosmic Bean, Brody had been one of the guys who'd helped paint the place and do some other repairs. But none of the other guys who'd assisted had hung around after the work was done. They now came in for coffee and a sandwich once in a while, but that was it.

Sighing, she knew she owed them all a debt of gratitude—Brody, Travis Gentry and his brothers, Josh and Griff, Ed Torberg, even the sheriff, and when Brody started hanging around, she'd thought it was because of the friendship they'd formed. Brody had just broken up with his girlfriend, and Serena, as a friend, had been there to listen. It had been nice for her to have a good friend, but that was all it had ever been.

The door opened and Regina Gentry walked in. “Hey, Serena.”

“Hi, Ginny,” Serena said, realizing she couldn’t stay in the ladies’ room any longer. She’d long ago gotten over the fact that Ginny had been with Cole that night.

With a toss of her head, Ginny flicked her long dark hair behind her shoulders. “It’s really cool that Cole’s back, isn’t it?”

It took a moment for Serena to respond. “Um, yeah, it’s nice. Ryan’s real happy about it.”

Ginny eyed Serena uneasily. “Would it… bother you if I went out with Cole?”

Caught off guard, Serena gulped. “Would it both—Oh, um, no, of course not. Why would it?”

Raising her hands, Ginny shrugged. “Just making sure.”

“Well, you can be absolutely sure,” Serena said, but the pang she felt in her chest told her she wasn’t sure at all.

“Oh, good. I know how you two were before and I just thought—”

“That was years ago.”

“Just wanted to be sure.” She beamed from ear to ear.

Serena managed a grimace of a smile. "Be my guest." She turned and left, unsure which direction to go to avoid seeing anyone. If one more person mentioned Cole or told her how she felt, or should feel, about him, she would scream.

No one knew how she felt. *She* didn't even know.

COLE WATCHED FOR SERENA to return the same way she'd gone, but ten minutes had passed and still no Serena. His booth was packed up to go, but he'd made a decision that when she came back, he was going to talk to her. Or at least, let her know that he wanted to.

Brody stood near the first-aid booth, chatting with Mac and Natalia, but he kept checking his watch. Maybe he was waiting for Serena, too. And if that was the case, Cole was unlikely to get a chance to speak to her tonight.

The music had stopped for a while because the band was on a break, but now they were tuning up again. Hearts On Fire was a local group he and Ryan used to jam with once in a while. But Cole's guitar playing pretty much sucked. For sure it wasn't at the level it had to be for a band member.

He hadn't picked up a guitar since he had left town, but when the band started playing, he remembered the feeling. It was like being injected with molten energy. Nothing could compare. Well, almost nothing. Making love with Serena had topped everything. More than once he'd wondered what that would be like now—with all the innocence gone.

His body quickly responded to the thought. Not good. He glanced at the small group of women who'd been hanging around his booth earlier and who'd asked him to join them later. He'd brushed off the invitation, but why not take them up on it? He felt like dancing, and dancing with a stranger right now seemed safer.

One of the women caught his eye and waved him over. There were five of them, ranging in age from early to late twenties. The one who'd waved was around twenty-seven and she was attractive. But oddly, the hormones that had kicked in when he'd been thinking of Serena couldn't be revived. And now this other woman was walking toward him. No escape.

"Hi, remember me?" she said.

He smiled. She was pretty, with a great body, and she was about half his height. Unlike Serena, who was close to his height and had fit perfectly against him. *Way back when.* He forced away the thought and focused on the girl. "How could I not?"

"This is a great song. Do you want to dance?"

He glanced at the now-crowded dance floor

and was about to beg off, when he saw Serena with Quint. Dancing. His chest tightened. She was smiling and laughing, looking into Quint's eyes. Serena was even more beautiful than when she was younger…in a more mature way. Sexy. Yet she still had that little-girl look about her. Maybe it was the curly, strawberry-blond hair, a little tamer now than previously, the freckles across her nose, though he hadn't seen if they were still there. When she'd helped him up, he'd been too shocked to notice anything but her eyes. Her amazing eyes.

He pulled his gaze from Quint and Serena and brought it to the eager woman in front of him. "Sure," he said. "Why not."

As they moved to the floor, he vaguely heard the girl introduce herself as Miranda Dooley. The dance floor was jammed. Everyone seemed to be dancing, locals and tourists alike, and everyone was having a good time. Everyone but him. Not that it mattered.

"How can you live in such a small town?" the woman asked as they began dancing. "Isn't it boring?"

"I lived in Chicago and found that pretty boring. I lived in California and found that boring. And now I'm here dancing with you, and it's much more interesting," he lied.

She smiled, and he tried to smile back, but

he couldn't muster much enthusiasm. And the floor was so crowded now he felt as though he was playing human bumper cars. Getting thumped from all sides, he attempted to avoid another dancer and stepped on Miranda's foot. "Sorry," he said. "I think I'd be just as happy to sit this one out."

Instantly, she moved closer, her legs molding against his. "No. Let's finish. I didn't mean *you* were boring. I just can't imagine moving *here* from California. I'd love to live in Hollywood. Or Malibu. Or Santa Monica. Or—"

"So, why don't you?" Cole's impatience surged. Just then Cole noticed Travis Gentry heading over from the other side of the open area, his expression as dark as a thunderstorm.

"If it were that easy, I'd be there right now. But it's complicated." Travis tapped her on the shoulder. She pivoted. "Trav. Oh, my gosh. What are you doing here?" she inquired, as if surprised. But for some reason Cole didn't feel she was.

"You know damn well," he said, before scowling at Cole. "Sorry, man. My fiancée is trying to make the point that I work too much." He grabbed her hand and began to lead her away.

Cole looked at the girl, who shrugged. "Sorry," she mouthed, and then the two walked off, leaving Cole in the middle of the dance floor.

The song was over, too, so Cole decided it was as good a time as any to blow this gig and go home. Just as he made a move to leave, he spotted Serena by herself at the edge of the crowded dance floor. She stood there watching and swaying with the music and then the song ended. She turned. Their eyes met.

Another song began, "Total Eclipse of the Heart." Everyone around Cole melted away, and his universe narrowed to one person. Time suddenly seemed suspended as, hesitantly, he took one step toward her. He held his breath… took another step, then another, almost in slow motion, until they were only inches apart. As natural as anything in the world had ever been, Cole extended his hand. "May I have this dance? I'd like to talk to you."

Blood thundered through his veins as he waited for her answer. Her expression shifted from surprise to puzzlement. Then, after the longest moment of his life, she accepted his hand.

It was warm…soft. An avalanche of emotions crashed through him. Love…longing. *Heartbreak.*

He felt a jolt as they came together, bodies touching in all the right places. But when he began to dance, she stiffened like an ironing board. He felt her hand tremble…or was it his?

The moment was awkward, not at all as he'd envisioned it only seconds earlier. But years had gone by since they'd even spoken. And that had been through a jail window. Of course this would be awkward.

They danced mechanically, and she stared straight over his shoulder, as he did over hers. "I've really wanted to have a minute with you," he said. "To…to tell you—" Someone bumped into them and Cole was grateful. She was here having a good time. So was he. To bring up other stuff was just…inappropriate.

She pulled back, waiting for him to finish.

Her tawny eyes were every bit as pretty as before, her lashes just as dark and long. And she did still have freckles across her nose. "I wanted to say…how surprised I was to see you living in Spirit Creek," he blurted like an idiot.

She frowned, pulling back a little more. "That's what you wanted to talk to me about?"

He cleared his throat. "Um…no, not really." But suddenly, with her so close, he couldn't pull up another coherent sentence.

After what seemed like half a century, she prompted, "What was the other thing?"

Cole had never dreamed anything could be as hard as this was proving to be. Talking about someone else was the easy part. Talking about himself was excruciating. He drew in another breath and regrouped. "Yeah." He started dancing again, but wasn't even hitting the beat. "Years ago…at the jail, when you told me how you felt, I said a lot of things. When I said, I didn't think it would've worked out for us anyway, that I didn't want to be married—it wasn't true. It was me hiding how I felt. I didn't understand, not until much later, what it must've been like for you. Whatever I said had nothing to do with how I felt about you. But you never returned and I never got to apologize."

He felt her flinch. Then she stopped dancing and pulled away. Her eyes grew steely, and she pursed her lips again. "*That's* what you wanted to talk to me about?"

"No, not just that," he said quickly. He wanted to tell her he'd give anything if he could turn back the clock. That he'd give or do anything to bring Celine back…to make Ryan a whole person again. He wanted to tell her he intended to face up to what he'd done, to do whatever he could to help those he'd hurt. *Tell her he'd never, ever, meant to hurt her.*

"I wanted to say I am sorry I was angry at you. It was stupid of me. I was wrong. I made a horrible mistake that hurt a lot of people. I live with that every day of my life, and I will for the rest of it. I wanted to say I am sorry I didn't—"

"You're sorry?" she spat out, her expression incredulous. "Sorry works if you forget to take out the trash, or forget an important date, or when you're late for dinner. 'Sorry' doesn't even begin to—"

She stopped suddenly and glanced around, apparently still as concerned about what other people thought as she'd always been. One hand up, as if to ward him off like a devil, she took a step back, then another.

A couple of dancers, strangers, halted and gawked, but the rest just kept on dancing. As Serena disappeared into the crowd, Cole felt someone bump into him on his right, then on the left as the ache in his chest grew more painful by the second.

He hadn't said anything he'd intended to say…what he needed to say.

CHAPTER FIVE

THE NEXT DAY SERENA drove down the long, narrow driveway leading to Isabella St. Germaine's home, pulled up near the porch and parked. On the way to the door, she wished she'd never signed on as a volunteer to help the church drive for donations to send to soldiers in Iraq, which Isabella headed up. But at the time, Serena hadn't given it a thought and had spent a half day each month for the past two months with Isabella and a couple of other women sorting and boxing the donations. Now, suddenly, the get-together seemed awkward.

She'd met Cole's mother a few times back in high school, but had never talked to her at length. Serena didn't know if Bella thought badly of her for breaking off with Cole when he was in jail, but if the woman did, she'd kept it to herself, and she and Serena had always exchanged pleasantries in passing. While Serena knew most of the people in town, the people she knew best were those who came to the café frequently. Bella had never once come in.

Serena had thought about bowing out of the church job, but then decided she couldn't stop living her life just because Cole was back. She had to get used to the idea and she might as well consider continuing this volunteering her first step in forgetting the past and moving on.

But was she? She'd waited to go to Isabella's…waited until she saw Cole's Jeep in front of his office and she knew he wouldn't be at his mother's.

Serena took a deep breath, knocked and waited. After a moment, she knocked again. Still no answer. Odd. She tried the door and it opened easily. She peered inside and called out, "Bella? It's Serena Matlock."

No answer. She called again, then walked in. "Bella, are you here?" She went through the living room and then to the kitchen. Bella was there, settling herself in a chair at the table. Serena quickly crossed the room to hold the chair for her. "Hi, Bella. I knocked and got worried when you didn't answer."

Then Serena noticed the older woman's short, graying hair was disheveled; and her sweater was askew and hanging off one shoulder. She looked a little dazed. "Are you okay?" Serena asked. She stepped back, and as she did so she felt something under her foot. She looked down. Bella's purse lay on the floor, contents scattered.

Bella waved a hand. "It's okay. I just stumbled and lost my balance."

Swiftly, Serena gathered up everything—a mystery novel, a cell phone, manicure set, breath mints and a set of car keys—chucked them back inside the purse and then set it on the table. "I can't tell you how many times I've done the same thing," Serena said, still wondering if the woman really was okay.

"Why don't you just sit for a bit. I can make you a cup of tea or…something else if you'd like." She noticed then that the other women weren't there yet.

"Thank you. That would be nice," Bella said. "The tea is in the cabinet right above the microwave. Make one for yourself, too."

As Serena moved about the kitchen, getting the tea and putting two cups of water in the microwave, she felt Isabella watching her. "Where are the others?"

"They couldn't make it," Bella said. "I was going to call you and tell you we're going to do it another time, but I guess I forgot."

"Doesn't matter," Serena said. "What day did you change it to? I only have afternoons after three when I close shop, you know. And even then, I have some other things going on."

Bella frowned. "I wrote the information down somewhere." A moment later she said, "On the calendar over there." She pointed to a calendar by the phone.

The microwave beeped. Serena fixed the tea, placed a cup in front of the woman, and the other at the seat next to her before going over to the calendar.

"Did Cole talk to you?"

Serena stopped and turned. "What about?"

Bella took a sip of her tea, then put the cup down. "About the business. Your brother's business."

"No. Why would he? Did something happen?" Serena drew out a chair beside Bella and sat. What had Ryan done now?

"Oh," the woman said, surprise in her eyes, as if she'd said something she shouldn't have. "No. Nothing happened. I just wondered how the business was working out for Ryan."

They quietly sipped their tea, then Serena rose from her chair. "Ryan hasn't said too much, but I know he was excited about Cole helping out."

Bella tapped the side of her cup, her gaze on Serena. "And how do you feel about it?"

The last thing Serena wanted was to discuss

Cole with his mother. She moistened her lips. "I just wish for Ryan to succeed. Haven't you talked to Cole about it?"

She shook her head. "No. But I'm hoping it works out so Cole will want to stay in Spirit Creek."

No way. Cole staying in Spirit Creek was the last thing she wanted. But looking at Bella, seeing the love in her eyes when she spoke of Cole, Serena knew what she must be feeling. The loss of a child, no matter how it happened, was heart-wrenching.

"Do you think he'd like to stay?" As soon as she asked the question, she wished she hadn't. Cole's choice to stay or leave didn't matter.

"Of course not. But I don't think he really knows what he wants. He feels I should sell this place and move to an apartment."

"And I gather you have no desire to."

"Not on your life."

Serena wondered if Cole, too, had noticed his mother's forgetfulness. That could be why he wanted her to move. To know was hard. Cole had always been able to let things slide off his back. Nothing had ever seemed to bother him. If something was wrong, he ignored it, pretended everything was fine.

All of a sudden, she couldn't help thinking of Beau, the name she'd secretly given their baby boy. Cole's son. Bella's grandson, she realized. The grandson Bella had never known she'd had. A lump formed in Serena's throat.

"It would help if you...told him," Bella said.

Serena shoved back in her chair and rose to her feet. Frowning, she said, "Tell him?"

"Tell him you're not angry anymore."

Oh, God. She almost laughed. *Not angry.* If they'd had a disagreement or a lovers' spat, she might be angry. But angry couldn't even begin to describe her feelings...or what she'd gone through that night and the next year and a half. But poor Bella wasn't aware of any of that.

"Don't you worry, Bella. Everything will be fine. Cole wants you to be happy, so maybe..." She shrugged, unable to finish. But she'd uttered her words with confidence. Cole loved his mother and wanted only the best for her. He'd talked many times about how he wished to make things better for her.

"He's a good man. But people just remember...before."

That was true. At least for her. "Things will work out, Bella. Just give them some time."

If only she could take her own advice.

She bestowed a fast hug on the woman, said goodbye and went to the front door. Eager to be gone, she stepped outside hurriedly—and ran smack into Cole.

"Whoa, there," he said, grasping Serena's shoulders to steady her. "Sorry."

"I'm okay," she muttered, and started down the stairs. Cole caught her arm.

"Look," Cole said, his voice thick. "You can't avoid me forever. Living in the same small town, we can't avoid running into each other."

She brought her head up and saw the plea in his eyes…the warmth that so easily sucked her in. To move away took all her willpower. "I'm not avoiding you."

He drew back, too. "You coulda fooled me." He smiled quickly, then said, "You made your feelings known the other night, and I can't blame you for that. I would just like us to be…civil. And maybe someday you'll allow me to explain."

"There's no point, Cole. What happened happened. You didn't return that night because you had better things to do. You cared more about your friends and partying than you cared about me and our future together. I understand that, and it's okay. There's nothing else to say."

"Except that it's not true. That night didn't have anything to do with how I felt about you. Nothing that happened had anything to do with how I felt about you."

"You might be able to convince yourself of that, Cole, but the facts are the facts."

He brought himself up, and she could discern anger gathering in his eyes.

"Just like that, huh? That's all it was to you." He clenched his hands, as if restraining himself. His lips thinned when he said, "I should've known, shouldn't I have? I should've known you have no room in your life for people who make mistakes. Guess I was too stupid to figure that out." He raked a hand through his hair. "I spent a whole year waiting for you to come back—or at least answer one of my letters." He scoffed. "Well, don't worry, I won't mention the past again."

She bit the inside of her cheek to keep her emotions in check. Still, tears began to well. In her heart of hearts she knew Cole wasn't a bad person. But he was who he was. Bringing herself up, she said stiffly, "Good. And you're right. We're both adults and should be able to live in the same town and be civil to each other." Nodding toward the house, she said, "I won't let it interfere with anything else, either." Then she rushed down the steps, got into her van and sped off, tires screeching as she did so.

Cole stood there for a moment, watching until she was gone. He'd come home because he'd wanted to make sure his mom was okay. She'd seemed preoccupied this morning, not herself. He had no idea what Serena had been doing here, but he was determined to find out.

He went inside and closed the door. "What's going on?" Cole called out. His mom was sitting at the round oak table in the kitchen, her head in her hands. "Are you all right?" he asked.

Bella nodded. "I'm fine. We just had tea."

He blinked. "Tea. Oh." He had no clue his mom and Serena were even friendly.

He was about to go to the refrigerator, when he saw a broken cup on the floor. "What the—" He strode over and started gathering the pieces. "What happened?"

"I bumped the cup against the counter," Bella said. "Right before you came in. I didn't have a chance to clean up."

"No big deal," he said. "I'll get it."

He retrieved the broom and swept up the pieces, then wiped up the spilled tea with a paper towel. "So, why was Serena here?"

His mom told him about the church donations, but all Cole could think was that it was one more opportunity to make an inroad with Serena. He had no illusions about anything. All he wanted was to explain, to… Hell, he didn't even know what he wanted anymore. He was tired of moving around, tired of being a stranger in a strange town, tired of not caring about anyone and knowing no one cared about him.

Yet there was nothing here for him, either. Except his mom.

He grabbed a quick drink and headed back to work. Ryan was out on a tour, and it was a good time for Cole to tackle the accounting system—rather, the lack of an accounting system. He paid some bills and went through insurance paperwork while waiting for his interview with a young man who'd answered the ad Cole had placed in the local paper for a part-time tour guide. After the interview, he'd have to take an older couple from New York on a two-hour tour to the seven-hundred-year-old Sinagua cliff dwellings.

He extracted a bottle of water from the mini-fridge, but he'd need something much stronger if he wanted to banish Serena from his mind. Though he hadn't expected to run into her, in a way he was glad he had. He knew where he stood. Yeah, he still had a litany of regrets, and he still wished he could make her understand, but he had to be realistic. She wasn't interested in his explanation…and he had to make amends, one way or another. Helping Ryan was the only way to do that. Knowing how much Serena wanted to see her brother succeed, he realized that by helping Ryan, he was also doing something for Serena.

The unique sound of a motorcycle, followed by a knock on the front door, interrupted Cole's thoughts. A young man peered inside. "Hello. I'm here about the job."

Cole smiled and motioned him in. The kid, who appeared to be in his early twenties, was tall, lean and darkly good-looking. Yesterday when the young man had called, he'd said he was new in town. "I'm guessing you're Sam Sinclair."

"You're guessing right." The kid flashed a giant white smile.

Cole invited him to sit and then asked some questions pertinent to the job. Aside from two years of college before dropping out, Sam didn't have any work experience and had lived in a half-a-dozen places since he'd left high school. "So," Cole said, "being new in town, why would you make a good tour guide?" Cole grinned at him wryly. "Besides meeting girls."

Sam beamed. "The girl part is cool. And I'd be a good guide *because* I'm new in town. Someone who's been here a while probably wouldn't find the work as exciting as I would," he said. "I think everything about the area is amazing, and I've read everything I could about it. I've gone on all the trails and some of the back roads, too. And even though I didn't finish college, I majored in archeology." He smiled. "Plus I've boned up on the history. Petroglyphs and all that. Were you aware there are two hundred and ninety-five ghost towns in Arizona and twenty-five underground rivers?"

Cole laughed. "Very good."

After that they talked about the hours, pay and expectations, and Cole ended with some casual conversation, a method he'd used in the past in business. It put people at ease, and they tended to reveal more about themselves without his asking direct questions. So far, Cole liked what he heard.

The kid shrugged when Cole inquired why he'd decided to live in a small town like Spirit Creek. "I didn't," he answered thoughtfully. "It picked me."

The answer surprised Cole. Either the kid was a lot deeper than Cole, or he was snowing him. Didn't matter, though. Cole figured someone with his engaging personality would go over well with customers. And Cole could practically guarantee that the girls would fall all over him. "Okay, Sam," Cole said. "You got the job."

"Really?" The surprised look on Sam's face shifted into a hopeful smile.

"Yes, really."

"Awright! When do I start?"

"How about this weekend? I've got four different tours booked."

Sam frowned. "Oh, I forgot to say I don't know anything about those vortex things, so one of those tours might not be good the first time out. But I'm a quick study."

Cole didn't know a whole lot about that particular tour, either, and he doubted he could do one. He simply wasn't into the energy thing. The only person he knew with any knowledge of them was Serena. "Well, there's the Internet and the library, and you might want to talk to the owner of the Cosmic Bean. She's knowledgeable, and the café carries some books on the subject."

"Cool," Sam said. "I'll check it out."

After agreeing on a schedule, Cole watched Sam as he climbed onto his old Harley, looking as if he was king of the world.

Cole sighed. So many years had passed since *he'd* had that feeling.

chance of becoming a grandma one of these days."

Serena's chest constricted. Her mother had never offered help or provided any moral support when Serena had been trying to figure out what to do when she was pregnant. Never offered to be with her when she'd had the baby, or had any empathy on the adoption. "You know what, I like my life the way it is, so you might as well put that idea to rest."

"What about that Romano boy you were dating?"

"That was a long time ago, so can you please drop the subject?"

"Okay," her mother said blithely. "Maybe Ryan will make me a grandmother."

"Maybe he will," Serena said, not buying into her mother's guilt trip. Ryan couldn't even take care of himself, much less a family.

Serena had barely gotten out the words, when her mother was onto another subject. Less than thirty seconds later, the woman said goodbye and hung up.

Standing there, Serena took a deep calming breath. In the distance, just over the mountains, the sky faded from red to pink to violet as it bled into twilight. Sky-blue pink. Nothing was quite as breathtaking as an Arizona sunset, and just watching the shifting patterns of light had a soothing effect on her. And right now, she needed soothing.

Then she saw one of the purple Jeeps rumble down the street and pull into a spot in front of the touring company, and Sam, the young man they'd hired, got out.

Sam had come into the café a couple of times in the past week, asking questions about the vortex-energy fields. He'd said he needed to know everything about them so he could conduct a tour, and he seemed to be an eager learner. She'd told him some things, but doubted he knew enough to do a tour. He'd also asked a lot of questions about the Gentry family. He didn't say why, but Serena figured it had something to do with one of the Gentry girls. He seemed like a nice kid, had a great smile and an engaging personality. If he'd been a few years older, she might've been interested herself.

Sam's engaging personality reminded her a lot of Cole's when Cole was in high school—he'd been easy to talk to, charming and a little mysterious, as if he was hiding something. That mysterious quality had intrigued her, made her want to know more about him, beyond his bad-boy reputation.

She remembered the exact day, hour and minute when Cole had asked her if she could help him after school with his math. She'd snapped at him, thinking he was putting her on. He'd stopped her after school again to plead with her. His sincerity had caught her off guard, and she'd ended up agreeing to "try" it once. She remembered her embarrassment the first time he'd come to see her at the trailer park. When she'd made an excuse about where she lived, he'd changed the subject, teased her about something else and made her laugh. Made her forget everything miserable in her life. And from that moment on, she'd been in love with Cole St. Germaine.

She smiled at the memory. She'd envied Cole his home and a mother who was always there for him, and he'd envied her having two parents. A real family, he'd said. Then he'd found out that it wasn't all it was cracked up to be.

Here she was, thinking about the past again. She glanced around for the TV remote, clicked it on and plopped onto the well-worn leather couch she'd bought from a consignment store—like most everything else in her house. To her, used furniture had charm and personality and made her home feel lived-in and comfortable. And dammit, despite what her mother thought, she liked being here…in her own home—even on a Friday night.

After clicking channels for fifteen minutes and finding nothing to watch, she checked the time. Not even eight. For some reason she felt edgy, as if she needed to do something but didn't know what. She picked up the phone and dialed Natalia.

"What's up?" her friend asked without so much as a hello. Natalia was the most direct person Serena knew. Some people found it off-putting, but Serena liked that quality. She never had to wonder where she stood with Natalia.

"I'm bored," Serena said. "What are you doing?"

"Just kicking back with Jackson." Jackson was Natalia's cat.

"I was considering doing something."

"Well, something is always fun," Natalia said facetiously.

"I'm thinking it should involve wine."

"I'm up for that. How about the Blue Moon? We could grab a burger and play some pool."

They used to do that a lot. Serena, Tori, Natalia, Liz Gentry and two other high-school friends had once been in a women's league, but then a couple of them married and Tori got involved with Linc and the whole thing just petered out.

"Terrific. I'll meet you there in a half hour."

Serena hung up, went to her closet and pulled out a burgundy sweater, a clean pair of jeans and her black boots. Then she went to shower. At once she felt invigorated, and realized that in the whole time since Cole had moved back to Spirit Creek, she'd been preoccupied, worried about how his presence affected her…and Ryan…and everyone else. What she needed was something else to think about. Something fun.

To shower, dry her hair, get dressed and walk down the street to the Blue Moon Saloon took forty-five minutes. The front door was open and honky-tonk music spilled into the balmy night air. Natalia was already there, sitting at a table at the far end of the room and waving.

A man sat across from her, but in the low light Serena couldn't tell who he was. She walked across the room, past the booths on the left and the tables that surrounded a tiny dance floor in the middle. A dark mahogany bar flanked the wall on her right, and beyond the bar in an open room at the far end was the billiard room, with two tables.

"Hey," she said to Natalia, then noticed Sam was sitting across from her. She eyed him. "Are you old enough to be in here?"

"Is twenty-two enough?"

"Yep." She smiled and noticed that the pool tables in the back were filled, which meant her group would have to wait if they wanted to play. "I'll get a drink and be back pronto."

"I ordered us burger baskets," Natalia said.

Ed Torberg, bartender and part owner of the bar, saw her coming and held up a wineglass and a bottle of red wine. "Yes, if it's Merlot," she said, then sidled up to Tom Thompson—aka TomTom—the owner of the hardware store, who was enjoying a bowl of chili. "Where's Pat tonight?" Serena asked.

"She and Benny went to visit her sister in California. So, I'm a bachelor for a few days." He winked at her. "I'm also testing the competition for the chili contest comin' up."

"Oh, that's right," Serena said. "I'll have to get out my killer recipes to see if I can take that prize away from you." Tom had won the contest three years in a row. "I'm thinking this might be my year."

"Not if I can help it, young lady. But you're welcome to try."

"Neither of you is going to win," Ed said as he handed her a glass of wine. "I've got a new recipe, and it's not the one you're tasting, Tom."

Serena had started hosting the chili cook-off at the café, but when Ed and Mac reopened the Blue Moon, it seemed appropriate to go back to the place it had begun. "How long have those guys been on the tables?" she asked Ed.

"Not long. If you want to play, I'll let 'em know so they don't hog them all night."

"Thanks." She went back and took the chair next to Natalia, who was wearing her signature black sweater, black pants, silver belt and jewelry. Her long brunette hair was pulled back in a sleek ponytail.

"Sam has a question for you," Natalia said.

Serena grinned at him. "More questions about the Gentry girls? I can introduce you, if you want."

"Hey, I want." His eyes lit up and a smile split his face. "But the question is about something else."

"Okay. Spit."

"I've got to take some people on a vortex tour Monday, and I've been reading everything I can about it. But I still don't get it. I don't think I can be a convincing tour guide unless I go to each place and get a real feel for it."

"That makes sense. You should do that."

"Yeah, but I need someone who really knows all this stuff, someone who's able to help me feel the vibe."

Serena liked Sam's intensity. "I understand what you mean," she teased, as if she had no idea what he was hinting at. "It's hard to get a feel for something just by reading a book."

He heaved an exasperated sigh. "So," he said, inching closer, "will you go with me?"

"Me?" She feigned surprise.

He sipped of his beer. "Okay, I wasn't very subtle, was I?"

Serena laughed.

A young woman, someone Serena wasn't acquainted with and who appeared as young as Sam, came over with their hamburger baskets, and Sam grinned from ear to ear. The girl blushed.

Once the waitress was out of sight, they all dug into their food. Sam turned to Serena. "Can you do it? Like, tomorrow afternoon? After you close the café?"

He even had that down. She smiled. "What about Ryan? Or Cole?"

"Ryan's got another gig and Cole knows less than I do." He gave her a puppy-dog look. "Please."

She sighed, then eyed Natalia. "Okay. Some people have been telling me I need to get out and have some fun, anyway."

"Cool." Sam frowned. "Is it fun?"

"Serena believes it's fun," Natalia injected. "But not everyone has her sense of adventure."

"Ignore her, Sam. She thinks bungee jumping is boring."

They all laughed and continued the banter throughout the meal. Just as they were finishing up, Ed walked over. "The guys in the back have challenged you ladies to a game."

"The guys?" Natalia turned to see and, squinting, she asked, "Is that Mac?"

Ed chuckled. "Yeah, he told me to tell you he'd spot you a couple of balls."

Natalia practically shot from her chair. "He said that?"

The bartender shrugged, palms up.

"C'mon," Natalia said, and yanked Serena from her chair. "We're gonna kick some butt."

"Oh, yeah," Sam chortled, and rubbed his hands as he followed the women to the back room. "Now we're talkin'."

Serena laughed, suddenly feeling energized. Mac had no idea what he was getting into.

But when she reached the table, she saw Mac's partner. Cole.

"Hey, ladies," Mac said. "Are you sure you're up for this?"

Natalia looked as though she was really considering it, then she said, "Sure. If you've got a C-note on it."

"Whoa," Cole and Mac said in unison.

Serena almost did a double take, but quickly regrouped, raised her chin, crossed her arms and said, "And you can take back those balls you wanted to spot us."

Cole and Mac glanced at each other, then Cole shrugged and Mac said, "Gosh, we'd hate to steal your money, but what the heck."

Serena was sure she saw a moment of doubt in their eyes—just enough to throw them off their game.

Each man pulled out fifty dollars and handed it to Sam.

Natalia and Serena did the same.

One of the guys at the other table turned to his partner and said, "I'm betting on the ladies." The other guy nodded and bet on the guys. Within minutes, word had spread through the bar and several other people had placed side bets. Sam demanded that those who'd made wagers and the rest of the people who came in to watch stay against the wall, out of the way of play. Serena knew most of them, but there were a few tourists in the group, as well.

"Okay," Sam said. "Let's do it."

Natalia removed a cue from the rack and rolled it on the table to make sure it had no curve. Serena did the same.

A low "Uh-oh" filtered through the group of onlookers.

It was all about confidence, Serena told herself, but with Cole observing her every move, her heart raced as though she'd just run a marathon. She'd never felt more nervous. Then some guy called out, "Hot chicks playing pool. Sounds like a great reality show." Then someone called out, "Work it, girls."

Serena couldn't decide whether to be offended or complimented...until she realized the extra advantage their team had. She went over, whispered to Natalia, then gazed at Cole and said in her most seductive voice, "Game on, boys."

Cole and Mac exchanged skeptical glances. Then Mac said, "Okay. Sam, flip a coin to see who breaks."

Serena got the break and, making sure she bent over the table with finesse each and every time, she proceeded to run half the table before she missed a shot.

Cole was up next, and in her peripheral vision, she saw him shake out his shoulders to loosen up. As he leaned down for his shot, Serena stood directly in front of him at the end of the table. She slowly ran her tongue over her bottom lip, then smiled.

Cole stopped, then wiped his forehead with the arm of his black long-sleeved shirt.

He was sweating. *Perfect.*

Setting up his shot, Cole mouthed something that appeared suspiciously like a curse.

Then he miscued the ball.

Natalia took her turn, also playing up her assets.

Blues music played in the background while the crowd cheered them on, hooting and howling on each shot. Cole went to stand on the opposite side of the table, his gaze sliding upward from her toes, lingering on her breasts, her mouth, nose, eyes.... Heat pooled in her belly. Even without looking at him, she could feel those eyes still on her. *Focus, dammit.* She breathed in and slowly let it out, watching as Natalia set up each shot. Without warning, Cole was standing next to her. Close. Her blood pounded in her ears. Then she realized what he was doing—the exact same thing she'd been trying to do. And, dammit, it was working.

Natalia missed the next shot and it was Mac's turn. Thank heaven. Serena went to get her drink from the table behind her and took a sip. Mac ran a few balls before, all too soon, she was up. As she studied her angle, Cole stood in front of the only real shot on the table, feet apart, arms crossed...a sexy smile that dared her to look at him. She took a deep breath... steadied her cue...and missed the hole by a mile.

Natalia strolled over and, under her breath, said, "What the hell was that?"

Her face hot with embarrassment, Serena grimaced. "I don't know."

"Well, I do." Natalia glanced at Cole. "He's psyching you out. Get over it."

She would. She had to.

On her next turn, Natalia raised her chin,

narrowed her eyes at Mac and then Cole. She moistened her lips. "This is it, fellas. You're going down." Within fifteen minutes the game was over. The guys demanded a rematch. Two out of three. And when the girls took home the money, the place was party city. Serena gave Sam a cut.

Natalia eyed Cole and Mac and smiled as though she'd just had fantastic sex. "Nice game, boys."

Mac mumbled, "Game, my ass. It was an annihilation."

"Good game," Cole grumbled. "Man, I need a drink." He glanced at Serena.

"Me, too," Mac said. "Ladies, do you want to join us?"

Serena hastily looked away.

"Can't," Natalia answered quickly, glancing at Mac. "I'm on call in the morning."

"And I've had enough," Serena swiftly said, and at that, both men went back into the bar. But Serena was sure she saw a gleam in Cole's eyes.

Cole indicated that Sam should come along. "You up for it?" he asked, and Sam hustled along with him.

"Well done, partner." Natalia raised her hand for a high five, and they went back to their own table. Serena had another glass of wine, but Natalia didn't.

"Oh, wow. That was great," Serena said. She felt more exhilarated than she had in ages. "I forgot how much fun we used to have. We should get a league going again."

"Yeah, like either one of us has the time. But a pickup game here and there would be good." She gave Serena a wicked smile. "Though I don't remember the league being so fun. I think the competition tonight had something to do with it."

Meaning Cole and Mac. As much as Serena hated to admit it, Natalia was probably right. "More likely the alcohol."

Natalia laughed. "Don't kid yourself. The heat was so intense between you and Cole I thought I might need a bucket of water to put out the flames."

"That's ridiculous."

Her friend snorted. "Whatever you say, kiddo."

"Man," Serena said, peering at her watch. "I had no idea it was so late. Isn't it time for you to go?"

"Yup. It is." She got up. "Just remember, you can ignore it, but it's not going to go away. You'll have to deal with it sometime."

They were almost out the door, when Sam stopped Serena. "Three o'clock tomorrow. Right?"

Natalia kept going. "See you," she said.

"Bye. Talk to you later." Serena turned back to Sam. "I'll be ready."

Cole ambled up behind the young man.

Leaning one arm against the door frame, a laconic smile spreading across his face, he said smoothly, "Great game, Serena. Any time you want a rematch, I'm available."

Her stomach fluttered like a schoolgirl's. Heat flowed through her veins.

Sam grinned like a fool. He obviously had no clue she and Cole had history.

Pulling herself up, Serena, too, managed a smile and said, "No, thanks. I like to quit while I'm ahead."

CHAPTER SEVEN

SERENA FLIPPED THE sign in the café window to Closed, then took a quick look around the restaurant while waiting for Sam to arrive. The mixed scents of coffee and scones, which she'd baked earlier, still hung in the air, reminding her of when they'd visited her grandmother in Oregon. She'd loved how her grandma's house smelled, loved the old squishy couch with lots of pillows and the ruffled curtains on the windows. Waking up to the scent of bread and cinnamon rolls baking in the oven had been heaven.

Nothing like her normal life had been, moving from town to town. Not until they moved to the trailer park on the creek did they stay in one place for more than a year, and that was only because her father had been arrested for drug possession again and went to jail again.

But Serena had already told her mother she wasn't moving anywhere. She'd stay here by herself if she had to. She smiled, remembering she'd put up such a fuss about moving because she'd started seeing Cole— The jangle of her cell phone broke into her thoughts. She checked the number. "Hey, there, Sam. I'm ready whenever you are."

He hesitated a second, then said, "Great! I'll be right over."

Hearing his enthusiasm, she was glad she'd agreed to go. It would be fun. She hadn't done the vortex trip in ages, and right now, it might be just what she needed. Though her mother had been lacking in a lot of areas, she's made sure the kids were educated about the vortex phenomena. Many people thought the energy fields were a lot of hooey, but from Serena's perspective, that didn't matter. If a person believed a vortex worked, then it would for that person.

Gathering her things, she considered bringing some water, but decided against it. If Sam was going to be a tour guide, then he'd better be prepared.

A horn honked outside, making her jump. That was fast. She grabbed her baseball cap and a black hoodie in case it got cooler. The sun was always warm in the afternoon, but the air could be a lot cooler on top of a butte or in the shade.

She closed the café door behind her and

reached down to lock it. As she turned around, she saw Sam in the driver's seat, with a red-, white-and-blue bandanna tied around his head—and in the back, Cole, wearing his Indiana Jones hat, tan safari shirt and jeans. His arms were crossed over his chest—and a grin spread from ear to ear.

"I invited Cole along," Sam said, rising up to peer over the top of the windshield. "He knows even less about all the vortex stuff than I do."

For a moment, she just stood there, her mouth agape. *Okay, Serena. Speak. Move one foot in front of the other and walk to the car.* Sam didn't know Serena and Cole had history, and she doubted he even knew about the accident. He was an employee, so for him to ask Cole along was natural. It was too late to back out, so she plodded down the steps to the Jeep and tossed her backpack with the maps and other information onto the floor in the front, then got in.

"This is really cool," Sam said.

She cleared her throat. "Yeah. Cool."

"Okay," Cole said. "Tell us where to go and this show is on the road!"

She'd like to tell him where to go—only it wasn't a vortex site she had in mind. If Cole had had any class, he could have told Sam no. He would have made an excuse.

"Just head toward Sedona, and I'll alert you when we're close to the first turnoff." She reached down to pull out her maps. "We'll go to Red Rock Crossing first. And while we're driving, I'll give you guys a rundown on the theory behind the vortex phenomena."

"How did you come to know so much about this stuff?" Sam asked.

Cole narrowed his gaze.

"My mother was a little, um, caught up in the hippie, transcendental-meditation thing, and we moved to this area so she could go to the vortex meditation spots, which a lot of people believe are connected with these mystical energy forces. As a kid, I thought it was a little strange, and when I was in high school, I decided to show her how stupid it was. I did a lot of research, but as I did, I realized the therapeutic value of the vortexes, and actually learned how meditation and biofeedback techniques can trigger the body's natural mood-elevating mechanisms. And that can enhance a person's overall well-being without the need for alcohol, drugs or any other mood-changing substance or addictive behav—"

She stopped once she realized how quiet the Jeep was, and when she turned to look at Cole, he was leaning back in the seat with his eyes closed. "Oh-kay. So much for how I learned.

Maybe it's best if I tell you about each place when we get there."

"I was listening," Sam said. "It's interesting."

"You sure?"

"Yeah. I like research. I studied the Native American culture of this area when I was in school, but I never learned anything about this vortex stuff."

Sam, with his headband, dark hair, dark eyes and olive complexion, could have passed for a Native American.

"Keep on talking," he said.

"Okay." She realized the road was just up ahead. "Turn at Red Rock Road. That's the next one on the left."

When they were on the road, she said, "People say that the drive down this road is a descent into the heart of Sedona, and Red Rock Crossing is the best vortex location for meditation. One of the reasons is the water of Oak Creek, which is supposed to help soothe and release hurtful feelings and assist in cleansing a meditator's aura...and spark new beginnings." She dug into her bag. "I brought a book for you that explains it all in more depth. That way, you can decide how much information you want to include in the tours. If it were me, I'd keep the talk to the basics and elaborate when the people ask questions."

She heard a rustling sound behind her, and then Cole suddenly leaned forward, his head between hers and Sam's. "Maybe I can hire you to do a vortex tour or two for the company, Serena," Cole said. "I doubt I'll ever be able to spout all that mumbo jumbo."

She was sure truer words had never been spoken. "Sam will do a great job for you."

After arriving at Red Rock Crossing, where she explained how vortex "sensitives" claimed each vortex strengthened a specific polarity in the body, mind and spirit, such as intuition, patience, kindness and self-confidence, they went on to the next site. She kept on task, detailing what she thought was important for Sam to know—masculine and feminine vortexes, negative and positive, magnetic and electric, and she even expounded on Native American medicine wheels, which worked in combination with the vortexes. Sam continued to ask questions. Cole, on the other hand, just kept watching her, his eyes riveted on her mouth, her eyes, her hands, and when he insisted on walking behind her, she knew exactly where his eyes were.

Nearly three hours later when they reached Airport Mesa, the last vortex site on the tour, Serena plopped herself on an iron-red slab of rock and kicked at the loose stones near her feet. A powdery puff of crimson dust floated upward over her boots and clung to her jeans.

She'd forgotten how relentless the sun could be and savored the respite offered by the shade of the gnarly juniper and rangy mesquite. Tired from hiking, climbing and nonstop talking, she sucked in a breath of pure mountain air. Not for the first time, the heavy scent of piñyon reminded her of the nights when she and Cole would lie outside on a blanket staring at the star-studded sky—and the stars used to look so close, she could've almost touched them. Nights better left forgotten.

Driving back, Sam said, "I can't imagine growing up in a place like this. Did you guys ever come out here to, like, party and stuff when you were in school?"

Cole laughed, his eyes latching on to hers. His voice went husky when he said, "Did we ever. We did a lot of *stuff.*"

"Some of us did," Serena said, turning businesslike again.

"You guys were really lucky," Sam said. "I froze my butt off in Michigan."

"That's where you're from?" Serena was surprised at the revelation. She'd asked him previously, but he'd just brushed the question aside.

"Detroit. But I got out of there as soon as I could."

Serena saw his hands tighten on the steering wheel.

"Hey," Sam said. "Are there any places around to pan for gold?"

"Yep. But it's a little west of here," Cole said. "Around the turn of the century, there was a big gold rush around Prescott in the Bradshaw Mountains."

"Silver," Serena said. "More silver mining than gold." She remembered how Ryan always dragged her along to pan for placer gold. Several times they'd found little flakes and chips that had washed down from the mountains after a rain or snow melt higher up. Serena smiled to herself. Tales of hidden riches in the Bradshaws had always fascinated her brother, and once, before she'd started dating Cole, she and Ryan and some other friends had gone into a couple of the old mines. She shivered just thinking about how dangerous that had been, yet they'd blithely gone ahead. No fear, no nothing. "There was a lot of copper mining, too," Serena said. "Near Jerome. That's one of your tours, isn't it?" She looked at Cole.

"Of course," Cole said. "Ryan likes to do that one and Sam's already more knowledgeable about the area than I am."

She agreed. He seemed to be. Inordinately

so. “What brought you here, Sam? Why are you so interested in the area?”

He shrugged. “It just seems like a great place, and since I was born here, I thought I’d check it out.”

“Really,” Serena said, trying to remember anyone with the name Sinclair. “Did your parents live here?”

“I guess. At least for a while. I was adopted, though, so I don’t know for sure.”

Serena felt a stab in her gut. He couldn’t be her son because he was too old. But there might come a day when her child would want to find her. Or Cole.

THE NEXT MORNING SERENA stretched to get out the kinks in her legs. She was stiff from all the walking they’d done yesterday. She kicked off the down comforter and glanced at the clock: 6:00 a.m. Plenty of time to have coffee, read the Sunday paper and make the early church service. Her parents had never thought much of going to church, and consequently, neither she nor Ryan had had any religious education. Not until she’d made her decision to give her baby up for adoption had she begun attending regularly.

Then, after moving, renovating the house and getting the café up and running, she’d gotten out of the habit, and now only went sporadically. But after yesterday, she felt a desire again.

She stretched, trying to decide. She could just stay in bed and do a crossword puzzle; only, she knew how futile that would be when all she could think of was Cole. And whether she should tell him about the baby. There didn't seem to be any point in telling him. So why did she feel this guilty?

Ridiculous. She rolled over, threw her feet off the bed and sat up. Lying here perseverating about things she had no control over was useless. She went into the kitchen, made coffee, took a quick shower and headed for church.

Afterward, she stopped outside for a moment to talk to Travis Gentry, the vet. She'd been surprised to hear he was getting married soon. "I hear congratulations are in order, Trav," Serena said. He was Serena's age, and the youngest of the three boys in the Gentry family. His sister Ginny was a year younger than him.

"We'll see," Trav said.

She looked at him sideways. "That's a strange thing to say. You're supposed to be excited."

"Have you ever planned a wedding?" he asked.

Serena felt a little tick in her chest. He didn't mean *her* literally, since he didn't know anything about her wedding to Brett and why.

"It's amazing anyone actually gets married after making wedding plans," he went on.

She laughed. "Everything will work out. In the end, you'll be delighted that you have something so special to remember."

"Travis." Serena turned to find Amelia Gentry, Travis's grandmother, barreling toward them.

"Uh-oh," Travis said. "I gotta go. Nice running into you, Serena."

Serena, too, was about to leave, when Mrs. Gentry came over. "Well, I'm surprised you're here, Serena."

Serena smiled, abruptly feeling compelled to explain why she didn't attend church more often. But her rebellious streak prevailed and she didn't.

"Considering your behavior."

"Excuse me?"

Mrs. Gentry leaned closer, as if what she was about to say was confidential. "At the festival. Doing things like that can be bad for business, if you know what I mean."

Drawing back, Serena couldn't believe her ears. But then she wasn't sure what the woman was talking about. The fight with Ryan? The dance with Cole, or getting involved in Ellen and Dan Fletcher's marital discord? "I don't know what things you're referring to. And my business is just fine."

Suddenly, Serena became aware that half the congregation had huddled around to watch them, including Pastor Donaldson. Serena gazed at the crowd and smiled. "Just a little fun discussion," she said, then turned on her heel and headed for the parking area.

Her blood pumping, she climbed into her van and decided to visit Natalia. She needed to vent and her friends were always there to listen. Except, Natalia was on call, she recollected. She might not be home.

She got in and started driving anyway. Natalia lived in a hillside condo outside of town, just a couple of blocks from where Ryan lived. She hadn't talked to him yet, either. In fact, she'd barely talked to him since Cole had come back and insinuated himself into all their lives. She'd go to Ryan's instead.

Even though her brother had said things were fine, she'd intuited that something wasn't right. It was the same intuition she'd had when they were kids. A sixth sense, almost. Like the day he'd fallen from the tree and hit his head. Everyone had thought she was wacky when she said that Ryan was in trouble. If she hadn't insisted on trying to find him, he might have died.

Lately, she'd had that same feeling. And the fact that Ry seemed to get riled these days at the drop of a dime didn't help. Maybe he wasn't all that happy with Cole around helping out. But if he wasn't, that was easy to take care of. Maybe the issue was Ryan's girlfriend. Maybe, maybe, maybe. She had no information from Ryan, but she knew in her gut something was amiss.

She picked up her cell, hit the speed dial for Ryan's number and listened as the phone rang and rang. Odd that his answering machine hadn't kicked in. Maybe he was working? She called Ryan's office. No answer there, either, but she left a message that she was trying to find him…and that it was important.

She was coming up on his street, tried his number again and after five rings he still hadn't answered. For sure something wasn't right.

CHAPTER EIGHT

"RYAN?" SERENA KNOCKED again. She tried to recall the last time they'd spoken. After the jazz festival, she was sure. But that had been a while. When he didn't answer the door, she decided to use the key he'd given her after he'd moved in.

"Ryan? Are you here? It's Serena," she said as she stepped inside, then immediately tripped over something in the entryway. She let a sigh of exasperation. Ryan might have changed in some ways, but he was still as untidy as ever.

"Ryan?" She wove her way around the mess and went into the living room, and as her eyes adjusted to the low level of light, she cringed. The whole place was a mess.

The blinds were closed, but she could see tinfoil on the windows behind those that faced west, reminding her how their mom used to cover the windows in their trailer to keep the Arizona sun from turning the trailer into an oven. She couldn't remember if that had worked, since winter was the only time the tin box wasn't hot.

She heard banging, then saw the arcadia doors to the small balcony off the dining area agape, blinds flapping against the frame.

Dammit, Ryan. When are you ever going to be responsible?

Resignedly, she crossed the room to shut the sliding door, and as she did, she had the oddest feeling. The apartment was excessively messy. Empty pizza boxes, beer bottles and half-filled chip bags were strewn on the floor, the counters, even the couch.

She swung around, glancing from one side of the room to the other. Mess everywhere. And the dust on the furniture she could've written her name on it. She sucked in a deep breath. Ryan's laziness had gotten worse.

Disappointment switched to anger, then weariness settled in her chest. More than once she'd wanted to let Ryan sink or swim on his own. All the experts said that was what she should do. Her friends said it; even her mother had said it. Serena had done that once and it had almost cost Ryan his life. Years ago when they'd lived in Phoenix, at Brett's urging, she'd told Ryan she couldn't help him anymore. He'd simply gotten worse, and after he was evicted from his apartment, he'd been homeless. She hadn't known until he was in the hospital with hepatitis. He'd almost died, and if he had… She shook her head. No way. She'd never do it again.

She picked up a couple of pizza boxes and took them to the kitchen. As she set them on the counter, a strange feeling washed over her and the hair on the back of her neck prickled. She wasn't alone. She whirled. A man stood silhouetted in the open doorway. She screamed. In the same instant, she recognized the hat.

Cole. "Oh, God!" she spat. "You scared me half to death."

"Sorry." He sauntered in. "The door was ajar and I thought someone might be burglarizing the place."

Her hands shook as she attempted to stuff some pizza boxes in the trash, but the garbage can was too full to take any more. She went back into the living room and grabbed a couple of tins from the floor. Struggling to act nonchalant, she asked, "What are you doing here?" She stopped, put her hands on her hips and glanced around again. If she cleaned up the apartment, it would just end up the same way again.

"Trying to find Ryan. He took some people out yesterday and hasn't come back." He frowned. "I figured he just went home afterward, or decided to go somewhere else when he was done. But when he didn't show today and I couldn't get him on the phone—" He shrugged. "I figured he'd call if something happened, but he hasn't, so I didn't know what to think, and then I heard your message and came over to find Ryan."

She didn't know what to think, either. In the past, Ryan had disappeared for days; once he was gone a week. Her hair had flopped down in her face when she'd bent over, so she pushed it back. "Well, he's not here, and I haven't talked to him." Her nerves tensed. "Did he say which tour he was doing?"

"The Jerome, and I think Montezuma's Castle."

"Those are pretty safe trips. And Ryan being Ryan, I find it hard to get too concerned."

Cole frowned. "What do you mean?"

His response surprised her. "You're good friends. You know how he is."

He shook his head. "No, I don't. How is he?"

What was he saying? Cole knew exactly what Ryan was like. Or at least, he used to. "Doesn't matter. I just thought…hoped he might be different with you working there."

He looked even more surprised. "Oh? In what way?"

"I—I'm not sure. I just thought he'd—" She shook her head, suddenly not wanting to say what she thought. Expressing her feelings seemed intimate, somehow. And she and Cole weren't.

Ryan had always idolized Cole. Had wanted desperately for Cole to like him, think of him as his equal. She could see why. Cole was a man's man, every bit the gun-slinging cowboy and polished businessman rolled into one. He'd shoved his hat to the back of his head and his dusty-blond hair appeared purposefully messy, just like some of the models' in *GQ* magazine. Except Cole would never spend time pampering himself. Besides, his hair had looked much the same thirteen years ago, before messy hair had become popular.

"I think we should report him missing," Cole insisted. "Get someone to begin searching for him."

She sighed. "This isn't unusual, Cole. He's done this so many times I want to wring his neck. I'd just thought that with you here, he was starting to get his act together."

But don't take that as a compliment.

Cole's eyes were riveted to hers and she felt compelled to get the hell out of there. She waved a hand to dismiss the subject. "Maybe he just seemed better to me because I wanted him to be."

Cole said, "We shouldn't leave Ryan's return to chance. What if the Jeep broke down? You know phone reception is bad in the mountains."

The switchbacks through Oak Creek Canyon and those near Jerome *were* some of the steepest and most treacherous if someone wasn't paying attention. "What about the people he took along? You must have a number where they can be reached, a credit card with their names. You could call to see if they got home."

He kept staring at her, his gaze traveling from her head to her toes, lingering on certain parts, then slowly rising again until his cool blues honed in on her mouth. He moistened his lips.

Her stomach clenched.

"I could," he finally said, then gave her a sheepish grin. "Dumb of me not to think of it."

"Good," she quickly said. "Will you let me know?"

He tipped his hat. "Why, I'd be happy to, ma'am."

Her cheeks warmed. She turned away. "Thanks. I'm going to clean up a bit here. Just leave a message on my phone at the café, will you?" She hoped he got the message to leave. *Now.*

He grinned. "Sure thing, kiddo." Then he pivoted and, as he left, said over his shoulder, "I'll be in touch."

She slammed the door and leaned against it, blood pumping hot through her veins. What was it about him that got her so flustered? So…hot. Whatever it was, she wasn't going to let it get the best of her.

She went back into the kitchen, got out a plastic garbage bag, grabbed some trash and jammed it inside. She'd filled one bag and started another, when she heard something behind her.

"You checking up on me?"

Serena jumped. Looking up, she saw Ryan standing in the entryway, his clothes torn and dirty, blood on his face. A motley-looking guy, one she'd seen at the jazz festival, stood behind him. "Ryan, what on earth—"

She started to rush over to him, but slowed when Ryan said something to the other man and the guy's eyes shifted to her. The two exchanged a couple more words, but their voices were so hushed she couldn't make out what was being said. Then the other man left.

"Are you okay?" She went over and touched her brother's cheek. "What happened? Where have you been?"

"Stop it." Ryan jerked away. "I'm fine. I just had an accident."

"An accident?" Serena hurried to the bathroom to get a towel. "What kind of accident?" Finding no clean towels, she took the least dirty one in the pile, wet one end and went back to where Ryan was sitting amid the junk on the couch.

"It's nothing."

She ignored the comment and sat down next to him. "Here, let me see how bad it is."

He gazed at her, then began laughing.

Her nerves tensed. He was drunk…or high. "Dammit. Hold still and let me clean the blood off."

Ryan quieted while she brushed the hair off his forehead, wiped the scratches and then the cut on his lip. When she finished, she laid a hand on his arm and said, "It doesn't look too bad." She felt the muscles in his arm relax. "Who was that guy with you?"

"Nobody. Just a guy I met."

Nobody he wanted to tell her about. She couldn't keep from thinking the worst: a drug source. Ryan's prescription for painkillers had run out long ago. "So what was this accident?" she asked again.

"I *said* it was nothing. Now, quit hounding me about it."

Which meant it *was* something. In the past whenever Ryan was guilty of something, his first line of defense was angry denial. When he got like that, to say anything more was pointless. She pulled in a breath. "I'm hungry. How about you?"

"I ate at the taco stand outside Black Canyon City with Lucy." He laughed and shook his head. "Lucy is freaking crazy."

Ryan's so-called girlfriend was older than Ryan, but how much was hard to tell. No one really knew anything about Lucy Xantos, other than the fact that she'd blown into town about two months ago. There had been the usual speculation among the locals about where she got her money, but no one was sure, not even Ryan. Or if he was, he wasn't saying.

Serena stood. "If that's the case, I hope you've stopped seeing her."

He leaned back against the arm of the couch and swung his feet up. Besides the cut and scratches, dark smudges lay like crescent moons under Ryan's eyes, and he looked as though he hadn't slept in days. "Crazy can be good," he said. "Fun. You should try it sometime."

"If that means getting banged up and bloody, I'll pass." She shifted position, crossed her arms. "I have plenty of fun." Playing pool the other night had been fun. Sparring with Cole—that had been fun. Going on the vortex tour had been fun.

Ryan shrugged. "It's your life."

"It is, and it's not up for discussion."

"Ditto." He grinned as though he'd put one over on her.

"Is Lucy still living at her sister's?" she

asked, hoping to change the subject. Lucy lived in a small cabin on her sister's property outside of town in an area that wasn't well populated. Her sister and husband were quiet people who kept to themselves. No one knew for sure what they did for a living, either.

"Yeah, she is, but not for long."

Ryan faced Serena and she saw his right eye was beginning to swell.

"She wants to move in here with me."

"What?" Serena jerked back. "That's ridiculous!" When he didn't say more, she reminded him, "The lease specifically states one person. You." Serena had cosigned for Ryan and had already ended up paying part of his rent to keep from damaging her own credit rating.

"I told her that."

"Good. Then there's no problem." She bent to pick up an empty chip bag.

"Don't do that." Ryan jumped up and snatched the bag from her. "I'll get it later." He placed a hand on her arm and urged her toward the door. "You can't come over and clean up for me all the time."

She gave him an incredulous look. "Since when?"

"Since now. Lucy says I need to cut the ties."

Serena's mouth dropped open. "Lucy says—" The muscles across her shoulders instantly contracted. What could the girl possibly know about Serena's relationship with her brother? Lucy didn't know how Ryan counted on Serena, needed her. That they had a connection few people did. Serena flicked back her hair. "Nice that she knows you so well already. What's it been—a whole month?"

"It doesn't matter. We love each other," he said.

She nearly choked. "Love? You've barely met."

His lips pinched, and she could tell she'd said the wrong thing. Again.

"Lucy was right. You don't understand. You don't understand anything." His face got red anew, then he walked over and held open the door.

As a kid, Ryan had had little control over his anger, and though he'd learned to manage it over the years, she always felt it was still there, simmering, ready to erupt. She couldn't let him make such a foolish mistake. "Maybe I don't. But I'm only thinking of you, and every time I ask something about her, you get defensive."

"I'm not defensive!" he blustered. "I know Lucy. And she knows me, and we want to be together. But you wouldn't have a clue about that, because every guy you've been with can't wait to get away. What does that tell you? Huh?"

She stared at him, aghast, then a horrible hollowness engulfed her. If he'd slapped her in the face, it couldn't have hurt worse. "We—we better stop. This…this isn't getting us anywhere." She fought the tears welling in eyes. "I came over because I was concerned," she said more evenly. "Cole was here, too. But since you've got everything in order, I'll butt out. But don't—" she shoved a hand through her hair "—don't expect me—" Her throat closed. She started for the door, tears clouding her vision.

"You just don't understand—" Ryan followed her. "You don't ever understand, and you never give me credit for anything. You're always expecting the worst."

She stopped abruptly and spun around. "That's so not true. I've always wanted the best for you. Always tried to make things easier. Every time you told me you would do something, I trusted you, and I'd get my hopes up that you were going to come through. And every time—" She halted. What was the use? Nothing she said would change anything. It never did.

She was tired, tired of feeling responsible. Tired of being unable to make a difference. Tired of being the bad guy. Then, as she gazed at Ryan, saw his frustration, his inability to comprehend what he was doing to his life, she felt like a jerk. All she was thinking about was how his problems affected *her.* This wasn't about her. It wasn't Ryan's fault he was dyslexic. He didn't ask for parents who barely knew they had children, parents who were gone more than they were around. Parents who never gave him so much as a hug.

Unclenching her hands, she was about say she was sorry, when Ryan reached out and slammed the door in her face.

AT THE CAFÉ, SERENA refilled condiment jars, wrote down the new special for the next day, which was just a different type of scone or muffin. Between her conversation with Mrs. Gentry at church, then with Ryan, she'd had enough testy encounters for one day, and called Natalia to talk, but she was out on a call. Serena thought about phoning Tori, but the last thing she felt like doing was sitting around with a happy couple who'd soon be leaving on a trip to Paris.

Seeing the sheriff's cruiser pull up, she couldn't imagine why he'd be there, since he knew she was closed on Sundays. She went over and unlocked the door. "Hi," she said as he entered. "What brings you by this morning, Karl?"

He stayed near the door, his expression serious. “Nothing, I hope.”

“Well, c’mon in,” Serena said, swinging open the door. “I’ll give you a cup of coffee. My private stock.”

He raised a hand to stop her. “No, thanks.”

“So is work what brings you here?”

He shifted feet. “In a way. You probably heard about all the problems Arizona has with illegal substances coming across the border.”

She nodded. “Everyone has, Karl. Is there a problem here, in Spirit Creek?”

“I’m not saying there is or there isn’t, but as an officer of the law, I’ve got to uphold the law and do what I have to.”

“Of course you do.” She folded her arms across her chest. “I don’t mean to sound dense, Karl, but if you’ve got something to tell me, I’d appreciate it if you’d just come out and say it.”

He hiked up his gun belt, moved over to the window and gazed down the street to the Purple Jeep Touring Company. “Well, I don’t have somethin’ to tell you. But I have seen Ryan hanging out with some sleazy characters lately.”

Did he believe Ryan was involved in smuggling drugs? “Ryan’s done some stupid things, Sheriff, but drug running isn’t one of them. I know Ryan. He’d never do anything like that.”

But she wasn't sure. She wasn't sure about anything where Ryan was concerned. He used to be charming and fun to be around most of the time. Now, he was angry at the world almost all the time.

Karl raised a hand. "Not sayin' he is. Nope, I'm not sayin' anything like that. I'm just looking out for the community, and wanted to tell you that if you notice anything suspicious, be sure to let me know. I'm not the only one watching around here. State police have been around, asking lots of questions. Asking about new people in the area." He moved back to the entryway and opened the door to leave.

Serena started to say something, then stopped. Everyone was aware of the drug trafficking across the Arizona–Mexico border and the illegal immigration, the "coyotes" smuggling truckloads of people across the border for exorbitant amounts of money and leaving many to die in the desert. But that stuff happened around Phoenix and Tucson, big cities a hundred miles from their little town. It didn't happen in Spirit Creek.

And certainly not with people she knew. Least not her brother. An addiction to prescription drugs was a far cry from running drugs.

The sheriff placed a hand on her shoulder. "You let me know if you hear anything. Okay?"

She nodded. "Of course."

As the sheriff drove away, Serena glanced down the street, saw one of the touring-company Jeeps pull in, then four people and the driver get out. Sam. He was new in town. So was Cole. So was Lucy, Ryan's girlfriend. Her family, too.

Did that make any of them drug smugglers? If that wasn't ridiculous, she didn't know what was.

activities as some people were, and she hoped he wouldn't be there.

"I may make it, or I may not. If I do, can we get together to talk?"

"Not a good idea. I'll be really busy helping out. I can call you back some other time."

"You won't, though," he said abruptly, and hung up.

She held out the phone, momentarily surprised. But at least that was the end of it. Usually a guy was gone after the first no. She punched in Ryan's number, but got the machine once more. "It's me again, Ryan. Call me, will you, please?" He sounded happy and upbeat the last time she spoke to him, but ever since the sheriff had been there, she'd been worried about him. She'd had the same anxious feeling that something wasn't right. She shook off the thought. She didn't want to think negatively about Ryan and was going to make a conscious effort not to. Then she went back upstairs and took a quick shower.

No sooner had she got dressed than Natalia and Tori were knocking at the side door. "Hey, ladies," she said, then motioned them to follow her upstairs. "I've got wine and appetizers first."

"I'm starved," Natalia said. "I did a canyon rescue for five people who somehow lost their boat on the Colorado River. It's unbelievable sometimes how people can get themselves into such predicaments."

"Amazing," Tori said. "I don't know how many times I've seen on the news that people are warned about driving in a wash during a storm. Yet they do it anyway."

"People think they can handle things," Natalia said. "They don't see anything dangerous and have a false sense of security. It's usually the younger crowd, though. These people were seniors."

Because the kitchen was downstairs, Serena had revamped a small alcove upstairs to resemble a tiny Paris bistro. The little room had a wet bar, a small refrigerator, a wine rack and a tall table and chairs. Quint had hooked up a sound system. She could really set the mood if she put on some French music. Mostly, though, she played folk, country music and pop, and had earlier put in a Brandi Carlile CD.

Natalia picked up a bottle of wine. "Want me to pour?"

"Do it," Serena said as she got out some artichoke dip and flatbread. "I made this today so you could test it for me. I'm thinking of offering an appetizer menu along with lunch."

"Great. Now, tell us what's going on with you and Cole," Natalia said.

Serena scoffed. “Nothing. Why would you think anything was going on?”

Tori and Natalia exchanged glances. “You spent a whole day with him, didn’t you?”

“Sheesh.” She accepted the wine Natalia offered. “I spent an afternoon showing Sam the vortex sites and Cole happened to come along.” She shrugged. “That’s it.”

“What I want to know is what’s going on with you and Mac?” Serena said, throwing the question back at her friend.

“He works with me. That’s it.”

Tori waggled her eyebrows.

Tori looked amazing, Serena thought. Since meeting Linc, she’d gone back to highlighting her hair and now wore contacts most of the time, instead of glasses. She really was back to being her old self, after enduring some tough times. “A likely story,” Serena teased.

“Is Mac okay?” Tori asked. “Linc said he has some issues about something that happened in Iraq. Do you know what they are?”

Natalia appeared surprised. “No. I haven’t heard a thing.” She raised her glass for a toast, and they all clinked glasses.

They yakked on like that for two hours before they realized they hadn’t even sampled the chili yet. Serena went down and brought up the two pots, then put a sample of each in two bowls. Tori said the first one was better and Natalia said the second one was.

"You'll have to get someone to do a taste-off," Natalia said, her words a little slurred. "Brody. You can get him to do it." Then she gazed at Tori. "We haven't discussed him yet," they said in unison.

"And we're not going to. He's out."

So they talked about Linc and and Mac and Cole and Sam and Ryan and Brody, and decided that everyone was screwed up in some way or another. But in the end, Serena knew it was only her. Tori and Linc were a great couple, and Natalia was so centered and so confident in what she wanted and how to get it. Serena had thought she knew what she wanted—a safe and secure home, an average *Father Knows Best* kind of family life and her café—but she was finding out quickly that maybe it wasn't. If it was, she'd have married Brody and been done with it.

By the time her friends left, Serena was no closer to figuring out what chili to take along…or anything else, for that matter.

But the next morning, she saw things clearly. Her life was great. She had wonderful friends, lived in a town in which people cared about one another. She was even getting used to crossing paths with Cole now and again. She decided right then there was no reason to make problems where there weren't any.

Maybe she and Cole could be friends… distant friends. As long as she kept her secret. Because if she didn't, if he ever found out, he would never speak to her again. She knew that as well as she knew her own name.

"OKAY, LADIES AND gentlemen," Ed Torborg said. "Line up on the right."

Ed stood behind the old wood bar like a barker at the state fair, trying to talk over all the noise and the country music playing in the background. A large sign in red and yellow hung above the bar, announcing the Tenth Annual Chili Cook-off. Chinese lanterns shaped like red chili peppers crisscrossed the high-ceilinged rooms. On top of the bar were ten or twelve pots of chili of different colors and consistencies. Some had little chili-pepper signs designating the hotness—from one chili pepper to five, and after that flames. Smaller bowls of diced green onion, cheese and crackers took up the rest of the space on the bar.

"Everyone make sure you have the sheet of paper that has the numbers on it," Ed went on. "Each pot has a number. As you taste one chili, you give it a rating from one to ten next to the pot's number. There are extra stars for some that you think go over the top. But you can only use up to three stars on the whole sheet. The prize is over there." He pointed to a giant gold-plated chili pepper with names of past winners written on the sides. The winner got to keep the pepper until the next contest. "Beer is in the keg. This is a help-yourself night." He raised his hands. "So, go to it."

Serena smiled; then, while everyone sidled up to the bar for chili, she grabbed a beer and sat in the end booth with Travis and Natalia. "So where's your fiancé tonight, Trav?" Natalia asked.

He shrugged. "Something came up."

Serena frowned. She had a feeling Travis was getting the runaround from Miranda Dooley, his intended. Serena had seen the girl dancing with Cole, and she sure didn't look like a woman who wanted to get married. "It happens," Serena said.

Just then Sam showed up and ambled over.

"I did the vortex tour," he said proudly, adjusting his headband. "And I smoked it. The people loved the tour and handed me a twenty-dollar tip." He grinned from ear to ear.

Serena gave him a fist bump. "Awright, Sam! Way to go." He was so cute in his camouflage shirt and safari pants she wished he was older. Not for the first time.

Sam turned to Travis. "You're the vet, aren't you?"

Trav nodded. "That's me."

"I met one of your sisters," Sam said. "Ginny. Is she coming tonight?"

Ginny was way older than Sam, and Serena hoped he wasn't looking for romance from the woman. Not to mention Ginny was a snot. Which Serena had known long before she'd heard Ginny had been with Cole that night thirteen years ago. Ginny had to be the most self-absorbed person on the planet.

"Nope. Ginny can't make it tonight," Trav said. "You're working for Ryan and Cole, aren't you?"

"Yeah." He stuck out his hand. "I'm Sam Sinclair."

Travis's eyes lit up like his smile. After a second, he said, "Well, good luck."

"Thanks," Sam said. "I heard you have a really big family, four brothers and three sisters."

Trav seemed surprised as all get-out. Serena was, too.

"Uh, yeah," Trav muttered. "How—"

"You're lucky. I always wanted brothers and sisters," Sam cut in, then quickly turned. "Hey, Serena, which chili is yours?"

She huffed indignantly. "I can't tell you that. It would defeat the whole purpose. No one is supposed to know whose is whose. That's why they're all in the same kind of pot."

"Ah. I get it." He shoved his hands in his pockets. "Okay, I'll check it out." He offered a peace salute and was off. At the same time, Cole walked in and slapped Sam on the back. They talked for a moment, then both went to the chili bar. Cole, dressed in jeans and a black long-sleeved sweater, looked directly at Serena…and smiled. Dimples and all. She continued to mull over what Travis had said to Sam. *You work for Ryan and Cole.* But Cole worked for Ryan, too. She wondered how long Cole would stay to help Ryan out. Surely he had a job to go back to.

Serena's phone rang. She didn't recognize the ID and her stomach clenched when she thought it might be Brody again. "Hello." She got up and went to stand outside, where it was quiet.

"Is this Serena Matlock?" a woman inquired.

"It is. Who's calling?"

"Lucy Xantos. I'm phoning for Ryan."

The knot in Serena's stomach grew tighter. "Hi, Lucy." She had no idea how Lucy had gotten her cell number. "So, why are you calling me? Have you tried Ryan's phone?"

"I did, and he doesn't answer."

Annoyed, Serena said, "Well, try again. He's not here." She clicked off and immediately felt guilty. She should've at least tried to be friendly. But her intuition told her Lucy wasn't good for Ryan, and the fact that she wanted to move in made Serena even more concerned that Lucy was using Ryan. They barely knew each other and she wanted to move in.

Serena went back inside and sat across from Natalia, who shoved back her bowl of chili and asked, "What's wrong?"

"Nothing that I know of. That was Ryan's girlfriend, Lucy. She called to see if I knew where he was."

"Do you?"

"No. But that's no surprise these days. The only person who's talked to him of late is Cole—or Sam." She shoved a hand through her hair. "It's as if he suddenly wants nothing to do with me."

"Isn't he busy trying to make the business work?"

"That's what he says." She folded her hands in front of her on the table.

"Well, there you go."

Right. But ever since the sheriff's visit, she'd wondered if there was another kind of business Ryan had going. As she glanced up, she saw Cole walking toward her. She'd been wondering the same about Cole.

Cole eyed the only open spot, which was at

a table next to Serena's booth, but before he got there, someone else slid into it. Travis, who was sitting across from Serena, made an excuse, stood and went off, which left two spaces at the table. "Do you mind?" Cole said, knowing Serena wouldn't make a scene in front of others. She might get up and leave, but she wouldn't make a scene.

"Go ahead," she said, and Cole saw Natalia's eyes widen, as if she couldn't believe what she was seeing. He didn't know Natalia well at all, but Mac had told him a lot about her. From what he'd heard, he could easily understand why she and Serena were good friends.

"Thanks," he said as he took the seat. He'd wanted to talk to her about Ryan, but hadn't known when to. This seemed the perfect opportunity. As much as he hated to rat out a friend, he thought Serena should be aware what was going on. He set his tray, holding seven tiny paper cups of chili and a beer, on the table. "Did you ladies vote already?"

"Serena hasn't," Natalia piped up.

"That's because I already know which one is the best."

"Oh, no. You have to taste." Natalia motioned for Serena to let her out. "I'll get you some."

"I'm not hungry," Serena said.

"You can taste mine if you want," Cole suggested.

"Just get an extra score sheet."

"Excellent thinking," Natalia said as she hurried off. Cole had the feeling she couldn't wait to get out of there. And he was getting the same vibe from Serena.

"This is good," Cole said. "Serena, it's time we talked."

The second the words left his lips, he saw her shoulders go up. "About Ryan," he added quickly. Though he had a lot to say about other things, too.

"Ryan?"

Just then the music ramped up. "When the song is over," he said. "The music is too loud. Let's sample the chili first."

She didn't answer, but appeared agreeable, so he grabbed a clean spoon from the bucket on the table that held plastic utensils and napkins and handed it to her. Afer sharing a sample of each, he pointed to number five. "This is the best. I don't even need to taste any of the rest."

"Yes, you do. It's not fair if you don't."

"Not fair?"

"Yes. You haven't tasted mine yet."

He laughed, and suddenly, she laughed, too. A silly little moment that broke the tension between them…and tapped into a cache of hidden emotions. Feelings he'd never had with anyone else.

He knew then that no matter what he'd told himself, he had never let go of his dream that someday he and Serena would get back together. His stupid-kid dream. And now he had to let it go, or he'd forever be living in the past. The music stopped.

Serena looked at him and said, "So, what about Ryan?"

He leaned forward, arms crossed on the table. "I know many years have gone by since I've seen Ryan, and I realize people change, but…well, his behavior just seems really off. He shows up late, forgets to do things, he has some really questionable friends and I've seen him popping pills I know aren't breath mints."

She kept looking at him, but didn't say a word, so he went on. "As Ryan's friend, I thought I should say something. And there is the business to consider. I'm afraid he'll do something to put it in further jeopardy."

Narrowing her gaze, she pulled back. Sat up straight. "In further jeopardy? He told me it was doing well."

"It is. But if he continues as he is, it won't be."

"I appreciate your interest in Ryan and his business, but what do you think I can do?"

"You can get him some help."

She sighed. "He'd never agree."

"You don't think he needs help?"

Glancing away, she waited a moment, then said, "I don't know what he needs. But when I figure it out, I'll do it." She turned back to him. "Anyway, it's really not your concern."

The skin on the back of Cole's neck prickled. "Really not my concern? How do you figure that?"

"Because you were supposed to be Ryan's friend and you blew him off for thirteen years. Now you're helping him out, but that doesn't make up for all those lost years. And when you leave—which could be any time, for all I know—he'll have to sink or swim on his own."

Her eyes sought his. "If you keep helping him, he's going to depend on you. He needs to be able to do it on his own."

"And if he isn't successful?"

She fiddled with the napkin.

"If the business tanks, he's not the only loser," Cole added.

She frowned, pushed back against the booth. "The only other loser would be Sam, and he has no plans to make this job a career anyway."

Oh, man. Ryan hadn't told her his mom had cosigned on the loan. He took a swig of beer and leaned back in his seat.

"It's really great of you to help him, but you're probably just delaying the inevitable."

He sat up straight. "Sounds like you don't have a very high opinion of your brother's abilities."

She glanced down, as if embarrassed. "I didn't mean it that way. I've been disappointed so many times I've come to expect it."

"Understandable. And also a good reason for you to do something now. Give him the chance to succeed. From what I see, he doesn't believe he can, so he sabotages himself."

"I can't force him to get help."

He eyed her. "Maybe you should do an intervention?"

She shoved her beer away. "Maybe I should go."

She got up and went outside, and heard footsteps behind her. "Wait, Serena," Natalia said.

She stopped just outside the door and recounted the whole conversation to Natalia.

"It makes sense," Natalia said. "Cole is around Ryan more than anyone these days. He knows what's going on."

"But I know Ryan. He'll just leave. It won't matter who's there."

"Even your mom? Cole's mom? You, me, Tori…Cole? We could all be there."

She laughed. "If you'd been here longer, you'd know that Tom wins every year."

He sat on a stool at the counter. "Nothing fancy for me. Just something to put into my cup to take along this morning." He held up an oversize thermal cup. "I stayed at the Blue Moon too late last night and I have two back-to-back tours if Ryan can't make it."

She turned. "What do you mean, if he doesn't make it? Why wouldn't he?"

He shrugged, shook his head and waved a hand as if to dismiss what he'd said. "No reason. Just…just a figure of speech."

Placing her hands on her hips, she stood in front of him. "No, it wasn't. What did you mean?"

When he hesitated, she said, "No coffee until you tell me."

"Okay. He's missed a few tours. I guess he's having some kind of personal problems. It's no big deal. I like to do the tours. More tips for me."

"A few tours. How many? When was the last one?"

He scratched his head, obviously wishing he'd never opened his big mouth. "It's all right," Serena reassured him. "You're not saying anything I'm not already aware of."

"He hasn't done any since right after I started. Cole and I handle most all the tours."

"And what's Ryan doing when you two are doing that?"

Sam shook his head again. "I can't say. I haven't seen him for days. He never comes to the store. But I think Cole has seen him."

Great. Just great. But why hadn't Cole told her last night? Even as she asked herself the question, she knew the answer. Cole would know she'd be disappointed—he was trying to spare her that. "Well, thanks for telling me." She took Sam's thermal cup and went over to fill it.

"Travis Gentry seems like a nice guy," he said out of the blue. "I like his sister Ginny, too."

She started pouring the coffee, but stopped and glanced at Sam. "She's too old for you."

At that, he guffawed. "Oh, man. That's so totally outrageous." Then he quickly sobered. "You, like, didn't think that, did you?"

Now she felt stupid. "No, I didn't, like, think it," she said, repeating his speech pattern.

"Whew," he said, then swiped a hand across his forehead in mock relief. "That would be too weird."

"Why? She's pretty."

"No. Believe me. That would be weird."

"Well, then you better stop asking so many questions about her. And the whole Gentry family, for that matter." She waited a moment. "Why are you so interested in them?"

He shrugged. "Is my coffee ready?"

She handed the mug to him but didn't let go. "You didn't answer my question."

Sighing, he said, "No real reason. They just seem like the people who kind of would know everything about the town and the people here. Like from years ago and all that historical stuff."

She frowned and leaned on the counter in front of him. "Stuff like who might've had a baby twenty-two years ago?"

He swallowed and his cheeks turned pink. Then he stood, fumbled to get his money from his pocket and laid a five-dollar bill on the counter. "Thanks for the coffee."

When he started to leave, she said, "It's okay, Sam. If it were me, I'd want to know, too."

He looked at her, his puppy-dog eyes filled with uncertainty. "You—you won't say anything, will you?"

She made a zipper motion across her lips. "Sealed forever."

As he left, she couldn't help but wonder who in town, besides her, had given up a child for adoption.

COLE WENT INTO THE KITCHEN, lured by the scent of his mother's strong chicory coffee. She was sitting at the table reading the morning paper—a familiar scene from when he was a kid, and one he remembered fondly.

"Good morning," she said.

"It will be as soon as I have a jolt of caffeine to wake me up."

"That's what you get for staying out late and partying with those rowdies at the bar."

"Excuse me? *Moi?* I was with the town's most upstanding citizens, and we were testing chili, not partying." The highlight of his evening had been talking with Serena, even if the subject wasn't the most pleasant. He'd been more disappointed than she was when she didn't win the chili contest.

His mother gave him a knowing look. "If that's true, this town is in trouble."

"Nothing new there."

She got up and went to pour him a cup of coffee. "That's a bad attitude."

"I agree. I'm sorry." He liked bantering with his mom, whose teasing always held a note of truth.

"Did you see Serena?"

He pulled up a chair. "What about?"

"About nothing. I just asked if you saw her." She handed him the cup and then gave him a quick hug. "You two were so close years ago, I thought maybe—"

"There you go, thinking again," he joked, hoping she'd take the hint.

"Would you like some breakfast? I can make some eggs."

"No, thanks, but I appreciate the offer. I've got a lot to do. I'll grab something later. But…" he said, hating to even broach the subject, since he knew how she felt about it. "I want you to think about what you're going to do when I leave."

She pursed her lips.

He quickly added, "I appreciate how you feel about living here, but it's going to get harder and harder to maintain the place."

She tipped her chin up in the same way she used to do when he was a kid and she wanted to get him to do something he didn't want to. "I'll find a roommate. Someone who knows how to fix things."

"Well, that's creative." He smiled. Actually, it wasn't a bad idea, but he doubted she was serious. "Well, think about it. I also feel you and Ryan should talk about selling the business as soon as it's back in the black."

She frowned then. "I don't think he'll want to do that. And it's not really mine. I only cosigned on the loan. It's up to him what to do with the company."

"That's not true. Your name is on the loan, and whether you consider the company yours or not, the bank does and you're still responsible. You don't want that on your shoulders if things go south again."

"But the company is recovering, isn't it?"

"It is, but Ryan isn't doing his part, and if he continues the way he is, I'm afraid that the same thing will happen all over when I leave."

Her eyes got soft when she looked at him. "You could stay."

Knowing how much she wanted that, he took her hand to soften his words. "Not an option, Mom. I don't want to spend my life taking people out on tours. I have a job in Chicago that I like." A job he hoped was still there when he went back.

"Then what is?"

"I don't know. I'm still trying to figure that out." He finished his coffee and got up. "Right now, I'm concerned about what you need to do. You'll have to make a decision pretty soon. I'll be happy to approach Ryan about selling if you want me to. Just let me know. Okay?"

"Okay. Let's talk to him together. As soon as possible."

"Great. I'll make an effort to find him and set up a meeting."

"Find him?"

"Yeah. He missed another tour yesterday, and I haven't been able to get in touch by phone."

"I'm sure his sister knows where he is."

He thought of his conversation with Serena the previous night. Wondered if she considered what he'd said. If Ryan did get help, then maybe the outcome of the business would be different, but at this point, Cole had no other choice. "Right. I'll phone her if Ryan doesn't show up today."

"She's done very well for herself, don't you think?"

He smiled and headed out the door. "Nice try, Mom. I'll talk to you later."

Getting into the Jeep, he had to laugh.

Every time he was around Serena, he got mixed messages. Desire, anger and bitterness all vied for his attention when he and Serena were together. The only thing he could be sure of was that whatever the emotion was between them, it was intense.

And that was far better than no emotion at all.

So maybe it was time that he called her on it.

"THANK YOU, DR. BLEDFORD. I'll let you know when I make a decision." Serena let the phone slide from her fingertips, then put it in the cradle. She couldn't believe she was actually considering an intervention. But after talking to two separate drug-abuse centers in Prescott, she acknowledged it was probably the only way.

She hadn't talked to Ryan in two days, and

he wasn't answering his phone. She couldn't possibly do an intervention if she couldn't find him. As she picked up her purse and sunglasses, the decision seemed to make itself. She'd find Ryan, ask him to go in for treatment, and if he wouldn't, she'd proceed with the intervention. All she had to do was get the people he most cared about to do it with her. Dr. Bledford had said either he or another trained professional would prepare everyone beforehand, as well as be there to facilitate the meeting. In that case, all she had to do was get Ryan to show up.

Driving through the parking area at Ryan's condo, she scanned the spaces for Ryan's vehicle. She spotted one of the purple Jeeps and his car, and knew he had to be at home. She parked, got out and went up the stairs to the second level, her heart pounding a death march in her chest with each step she took.

God. Why was this so difficult? The moment she thought this, she knew. She and Ryan had been so close for so many years that doing this to him was a betrayal of everything they'd been to each other. She'd been his protector, his confidante, the person he could trust to be there when everyone else had jumped ship. And now she felt she was his Judas.

Ryan would thank her later, the doctor had

said. But whether he did or not, she knew she could no longer do nothing.

When she reached his door, she heard music. Loud music. She knocked. Hard. A moment later, the door opened. Lucy Xantos stood there, one arm against the door, the other against the door frame—literally blocking the entry. The woman's dark brown hair was pulled back and Serena realized that under the makeup, she was probably a pretty woman.

"Hi, Lucy," Serena said. "I'm here to see Ryan."

Lucy moved to the side with an extravagant sweep of her hand, gesturing for Serena to enter. "Well, c'mon in," Lucy drawled in a purposefully husky voice.

One step inside and Serena knew it was a mistake to have come. The mess was still the same—maybe a little worse. Ryan was sprawled on the couch, half dressed, eyes closed. Two other guys were slumped in the chairs opposite the couch, and she was sure they were the same two who'd been at the jazz festival.

"Well, hello, pretty lady," one of them said. He had a Mohawk haircut, an earring in his nose, lip and eyebrow. Plus tattoos everywhere. Out of the blue, he shouted, "Ryan! Get your ass off the couch. You've got company."

The other guy, who had no hair at all,

giggled like a kid. "Yeah, you better wake up, because I might not be responsible for my actions if you don't."

"Shut the hell up," Lucy said, then she sashayed over to Ryan and nudged him with her knee. "He's had a long night," she said to Serena. "Give him an hour or so. He'll come around."

Serena went over and knelt beside Ryan. "Ry? Are you okay?" She didn't give a damn about the other people there or their threats. Ryan looked out of it, as if he needed help.

"What's he on?" she asked quickly. "He's not responding."

Lucy flopped down next to Ryan. "'What isn't he on?' is a better question."

Serena stood and pulled out her cell phone. No sooner had she opened it than Lucy batted it from her hand. It flew across the room. "You can't call anyone. We'll all be arrested if you do."

Adrenaline shot through Serena. She went to retrieve the phone, but the Mohawk-hair guy got there first.

"Ryan needs help. A doctor, maybe," she said, her heart banging against her ribs.

"Wh-what's goin' on," Ryan suddenly said, struggling to sit up.

Serena went to his side again. "Ry, tell these people to go. You need help and I'm going to get it for you."

Lucy stepped between Serena and Ryan. "Man, you're a piece of work. Who appointed you God over everyone?"

Serena was surprised at the tone in Lucy's voice, and her lower lip curled. "What did you say?"

Lucy inched even closer. Keeping her voice low, her face just a fraction from Serena's, she said, "I'm sorry if I wasn't clear. What I should've said was that Ryan doesn't want or need you to direct his life. He's a big boy. He's perfectly capable of doing it on his own."

Serena scoffed, narrowed her eyes. "Yeah. It looks like it." She turned to Ryan again. "Ryan, tell these people to leave."

He said nothing.

Lucy said, "Tell your sister to leave, Ryan."

They both stood there.

Finally, Ryan managed to say, "Go away, sis."

The hell she would. "Sorry. I'm not going anywhere." She crossed her arms.

Lucy went over to get her purse from a table and Serena used the opportunity to grab Ryan's hand and yank him up. "C'mon, Ryan. If they won't leave, then we will." She reached to put her arm around him and assist him up. And then Ryan said to Lucy, "You guys better leave. When my little sister makes up her mind, that's it." His words were slurred.

Serena felt Ryan move away, and then he flopped back down on the couch. “Leave,” he said.

The guy with her phone went to the door and said, “Let’s go. He’s useless anyway.”

As the others joined him, Serena held out her hand for the phone and after a moment, the guy handed it over. As she took it, he said, “You got cojones, lady. I like that.”

CHAPTER ELEVEN

SERENA SWALLOWED, bit her bottom lip to keep it from trembling. She fought to hold back the tears as she hurried to her car. After getting Ryan settled, he'd kept babbling about his friends and how much they cared about him. It hadn't been Ryan talking. He didn't know what he was saying. Those freaks who didn't give a crap about anyone or anything had corrupted him. But as she piled into her van and tore out of the parking lot, she couldn't contain herself anymore and let the tears stream freely down her cheeks.

Oh, God. Serena had to separate Ryan from those people before he got worse. Before he ended up dead from a drug overdose. It happened all the time. Heath Ledger, people you'd never imagine. Accidentally dead, but still dead.

She had to do it. Now an intervention was inevitable. She'd call Dr. Bledford and do whatever he said. Contact people was what he'd told her to do. Involve those Ryan cared about most. Because they were all to blame, the doctor had said. She'd resisted the notion. But in her heart she knew it was probably true.

She wiped her face with her shirtsleeve, and realizing that Natalia's was just a couple of blocks away, she took a right and headed there. She had no time to waste. Pulling into Natalia's driveway, she extracted her cell phone from her purse and hit the speed button for Natalia's number. "I'm right outside," she said as soon as Natalia picked up.

When Natalia opened her condo door, her eyes widened. "What the hell happened?"

Serena rushed inside. Told Natalia the whole story. Told her what they had to do. They began to figure out who most needed to be at the intervention. Serena, Ryan and their mom, for sure.

"What about Cole's mom?" Natalia asked. "Isn't Ryan closer to her than to your mom?"

"He was. I'm not sure about now. But he respects her opinion more than almost anyone's. Hers and Cole's."

"So, that's you, your mom, Cole's mom and Cole. Four people if everyone comes. What about Tori? Ryan's known her since he was a kid."

"But they haven't been close in a while. Ryan's closer to you now."

"Okay, me. That's five. I think we can all make significant points. And we've all contributed to his problem."

"You haven't. All you've ever done is try to get me to do something."

"Yeah. I didn't try hard enough. I didn't go to Ryan and tell him what he was doing to you. How he was not only screwing up his life but yours. And that affects me, too. Don't forget, I know a thing or two about people needing help."

Serena frowned.

"I spent four years in Iraq, remember. People do a lot of things under extreme duress. They need help when they get into trouble. It's not just when they come home that the problems start."

"You never said anything." Serena couldn't tell if her friend was talking about herself or other soldiers, but this wasn't the time to go into it.

Natalia shrugged. "I didn't. Maybe I should have."

"Okay," Serena said on a sigh, feeling a little better now that she had a plan. "The next thing to do is call Dr. Bledford and find out when someone can come out, then talk to everyone else to set the time and place."

"Will your mom come?"

"She better."

"And then you'll have to get Ryan to show up."

"Yeah. Maybe Cole will have an idea on how to do that."

AFTER GOING HOME AND contacting the doctor and everyone but Cole and his mom, she decided to first ask Cole if his mom should even be there. God knew, she didn't want to involve anyone who didn't have to be present.

She'd phoned the Purple Jeep Touring Company, and Sam had told her Cole was out, but that he'd have him call her. She'd stressed the urgency, and then, of course, Sam wanted to know if everything was okay. Once she got off the phone with him, she glanced at the clock. Only five in the afternoon. Lord, she felt as if the day had been a week long. She went to her wine rack and pulled out a bottle of Merlot. Natalia had said she'd call or stop by when she finished a couple of things she had to do to get ready for her next flight, so Serena decided she might as well relax until then. Going at the bottle, she wondered if this was how it started…a little at a time to relax and then you're hooked. But then, she wasn't Ryan.

Dr. Bledford had told her someone could be there the next afternoon, or the day after—Thursday or Friday, whichever worked best for the group. Her mom had said she'd have to drive all night to make the next afternoon, but surprisingly, she'd agreed to do it.

Serena took out a corkscrew and opened the wine, sniffed the cork as she'd learned to do in the wine-tasting class she'd taken the previous year, then poured a small amount in the glass, swirled, and sniffed again. Then, realizing how stupid and silly the ritual was, she laughed and downed the glass in one long drink. She poured another glass and went to sit on the couch. That was all she wanted to do. Just sit. And drink wine.

A knock on the door downstairs alerted her that Natalia had arrived. "The door's open," she called out. "I'm upstairs. C'mon up."

She quickly got out another glass and poured wine for Natalia.

Then she looked up and saw Cole. She jerked back. "Oh!"

"Is that for me?" he said.

She waved a hand. "You scared the bejeebies out of me."

"I guess. Seems to be my thing."

"I thought you were Natalia."

"Well, the message from Sam said you urgently needed to see me, so here I am."

Sam. What a devious little devil he was. "A little different from the message I gave him, but it's fine. I *did* want to talk to you and it *is* urgent." She handed him the wine. "I don't need another on an empty stomach."

He accepted the glass, then glanced around. "This is nice. I like it. Very…Serena."

She smiled. "Nice way to put it."

"It's true. You have a unique style."

"Unique? Usually people say it's eclectic. Or funky." She grinned. "It is what it is. For better or worse." As she said the words, she realized that in the space of a few seconds, all the tension had left her body. The wine had worked fast. She gestured to the couch. "Let's sit and I'll tell you why I wanted to talk to you."

He nodded and walked to the couch. "Okay."

"I wanted to tell you I was sorry I didn't listen to you about the intervention. You were right. It *is* necessary." And once she started telling him why, she kept on going, not just relaying the information about the intervention but recounting everything else that had happened earlier. When she finished, he held out the glass. She took it and drank the last sip of wine.

She realized then that as he'd listened, his expression had grown more and more serious, and now he looked almost angry.

"Bastards." He stood. "You're lucky to have gotten out of there. Ryan probably knew that, and that's why he told you to leave."

her chin and drew herself up on her toes. As if in slow motion, his mouth came closer, halting, hesitating; then, almost lightning fast, her lips touched his, and his lips touched hers. Just barely. They held the position for what seemed an eternity…until the urgency became so severe it was unstoppable. His lips descended full force on hers and they devoured each other as if starved for years. Her blood pounded through her veins and she couldn't hear a thing except the moan that escaped from her throat.

"Knock, knock." A woman's voice sounded from somewhere in the universe around them. "Anyone here?"

Natalia. Serena pried herself away. "Yes. I'll be right there."

"Should I come up?"

"Sure."

Cole smiled. He brushed the hair from her forehead. "It's okay. Just an emotional moment. That's all."

She ran her fingertips across her mouth. "Right." She walked to the stairway. "C'mon up. I was just getting some wine."

When Natalia reached the top of the stairs, Serena said, "Cole's here. I was filling him in." She turned and saw Cole sitting casually in a chair, legs apart.

"Hey, Natalia." Cole waved.

Natalia frowned at Serena while acknowledging Cole. She mouthed, *What's going on?*

"Cole and I were just setting up the plan. Here, have some wine and I'll bring you up to date."

Serena went over some of the stuff she and Cole had talked about and most everything else. When she finished, Cole stood. "If that's it, I'll go figure out a way to get Ryan to my mom's tomorrow."

"Great," Serena said, then started to walk him out.

"It's okay," he said. "I can find my way back down."

Standing at the top of the stairs, watching him leave, Serena felt an ache of longing in her chest, the likes of which she'd never ever felt.

WITH EVERYONE ASSEMBLED in Isabella St. Germaine's living room, the drug counselor trained as a specialist in interventions who'd come instead of Dr. Bledford, went through all the steps they needed to take and explained how he'd facilitate the process. Their goal was to get Ryan to agree to enter a rehab program. The person rarely agreed right away, he said, and he mentioned the things that could happen instead. By the time he'd finished, Ryan was due any second.

"I think we should go into the dining room

so we're not all visible when he arrives. Cole will bring him into the house, and then I'll go out, introduce myself and invite him in to talk to the rest of you."

"What did you tell Ryan to make sure he'd come?" Natalia asked as they went into the other room.

Cole shook his head. "Doesn't matter. What matters is that he shows. I told him something I thought would work."

"You feel it will?" Serena asked, staying behind with Cole.

"It better."

Just then they heard a car door slam. A few moments later, footsteps. Serena's heart hammered. The knock on the door made her jump. Serena hastily followed the others.

The entry faced the wide staircase that led to the second floor. The living room was on the left, it connected to the dining room.

Cole went to the door. "C'mon in," she heard him say.

"Is she okay?" Ryan asked. A silence followed.

"This is Bill Jessup, Ryan."

A second later, Cole walked into the dining room.

She heard the two men talking, then Ryan's voice getting louder. "This is bullshit," he shouted.

Then Ryan barreled into the room where they waited, Bella sitting, the rest of them standing. "Ryan," Serena said, rushing over to him. "Please listen. This is really important."

Ryan's face was redder than she'd ever seen it, the veins on his neck and forehead popping out. He stabbed a finger in the air directly at Cole. "You lied to me. You out-and-out lied!"

Cole looked to Jessup, who indicated Cole should respond. "You're right. I did. But it was the only way to get you over."

The counselor said, "They're here because they care about you. Care very much. And you might want to hear what they have to say."

Ryan stopped, as if suddenly taken off guard. But his hesitation lasted only seconds. He glared at Cole anew. "The only reason I came was that you said your mom was sick and wanted to see me." He turned. "I don't need this shit. I don't need you guys interfering in my life. I don't need anyone."

Almost before the last word was out, he fled out the door. Serena ran after him. "Wait, Ryan. Please wait. Just listen to what we have to say, and then you can leave and do whatever you want. Please." She grabbed his shirtsleeve.

He stopped, yanked his arm away and swung around to face her, tears filling his eyes. "You're a traitor. You're all traitors. All you care about is that I don't embarrass you, that I don't disturb your perfect little lives. Well, you don't have to worry about that anymore."

She grabbed both his arms to stop him. He wrestled free, then shoved her away from him. She stumbled backward and fell, but he didn't even notice. He was already at his car.

Cole ran toward the car, but it peeled away before he even got close. He helped Serena get up, then walked her back inside, his arm around her the whole way. "You did what you could," he said. "That's all you can do."

Inside, the counselor was talking with everyone, but he halted and took Serena aside. "This isn't the end," he said. "It's only the beginning. We have to give him time to think. When he contacts any of you, follow the plan. Say the exact same thing—that you're not accepting his behavior and if he wants to talk, he'll have to have this meeting."

"So basically, we're shunning him."

Jessup's mouth quirked up. "Never heard it called that before, but in a way, yes."

Serena grasped the logic, but she knew Ryan; the counsellor didn't. Cole knew him, but not the way she did. No one knew Ryan the way she did, and from how he had been talking, she was more worried now than ever.

"If anyone is feeling guilty for ambushing

Ryan, he's got you right where he wants you. He knows how to play you. I realize that doesn't sound nice, but there's nothing nice about addiction."

After they had all agreed to move in the same direction, the counselor left and they each went their separate ways.

To wait. To wait and see which of them Ryan contacted first.

CHAPTER TWELVE

WHEN THREE DAYS HAD passed without anyone hearing from Ryan, including Lucy, who'd called to find out if Serena had seen him, Serena went to the sheriff's office.

"What do you mean you can't help me?" Serena folded her arms across her chest. "I don't need help, Karl. I want you, and whoever else can, to get out to look for Ryan. That *is* part of your job, isn't it?"

Karl rocked back on his chair and shoved a thatch of silver hair off his forehead.

"Look, Serena," he said, leveling his chair and peering up at her. "No offense to your brother and your concern for him, but I've known him all his life. He does this a lot—goes off for days, even longer sometimes. We're a really small outfit here. We've got some important stuff going on and we can't go tearin' after someone unless there's good reason."

He glanced away, then looked down as if

embarrassed. "When an unmarried guy doesn't come home a night or two or three, that's pretty normal."

"But he said some things that made me think he might harm hims—"

"Serena," the sheriff interrupted. "Without any evidence that this time is different..." He shrugged. Then, in a soft, understanding tone, he said, "Why don't you go home and wait a little longer. I'm sure he'll turn up. If he doesn't show in a few more days you can file a missing-person report, and we'll get the whole county involved." He gave her a sympathetic look as if she were the one with the problem.

God. She'd never felt so frustrated. But another glance at Karl's square, set jaw told her that pursuing the matter was useless. Worse yet, she knew he was right. And if she got any other law officials involved and Ryan was doing something illegal, he could be in even more trouble.

Her stomach churned at the possibility. Then she realized she was doing it again. Protecting him. Maybe he needed to get caught. Maybe then he'd do something about it.

Yet despite all Ryan's peccadilloes, she loved him. He was a good person unable to cope. She stepped forward, then placed her palms flat on Karl's gray metal desk and waited a fraction of a second before she tried one more time. "What I'm really worried about is that something happened to him while he was scouting a tour. If his car had a problem or he missed a turn or something, he could be out there in the desert, and it's starting to get really cold at night." The scenario wasn't entirely unlikely. He could've gone to a secluded place to think and something could've happened.

Karl met her gaze and nodded. "Sorry, Serena. Come back in a couple of days."

Serena ground her back teeth. Okay. She had needed to try. Now she needed to do. She whirled on her heel and strode out the door. She'd gone less than five feet when an insidious uncertainty overtook her. She often felt this way when Ryan was truly in trouble.

As she took in the length of the street, the Purple Jeep Touring Company came into focus. She drew in a deep breath and sank onto a rustic pine bench propped against the sheriff's office behind her.

Where would Ryan go that no one would think to look for him? He didn't have money to hole up in a motel somewhere. And he wasn't with Lucy or anyone he knew. She'd already checked with some of his old friends, and they hadn't seen him in ages. One didn't even live in Spirit Creek anymore. Then she remembered the mines they explored when in high school. The thought sent a shiver up her spine. Most all the old mines were dangerous. But it was a possibility, and something told her it was the best one. When an urgent need to find Ryan slammed home, she knew what she had to do.

Transportation. She required reliable desert transportation, a good map, a few supplies and someone to go with her.

The terrain was far too dangerous to traverse alone, especially the remote areas where Ryan might've gone.

Only a four-wheeler could navigate the ungraded gravel roads, and even then, if she got stuck alone, she'd never get out.

Sam. Maybe she could get him to help her out. She picked up her phone and punched in the number he'd given her before they'd gone on the vortex tour. Somewhere between the second ring and the middle of the third, she felt a tightening in her chest, an awful gut-level fear. Pure raw emotion…an acute awareness that quickly became apprehension, anxiety and, finally, an all-consuming panic.

She gripped the phone so hard she felt the skin stretch across her knuckles.

The ringing stopped.

"Morning. Purple Jeep Tours."

"Hello, Cole?"

"Serena. Hello. Have you heard from Ryan?"

"No. Nothing." She didn't want to tell him how worried she was because she knew he'd just repeat what Jessup had told them. That they'd feel guilty. That they were responsible for Ryan's doing whatever it was. "I'm calling for Sam. Is he around?"

"Nope, he's out on a job. He won't be back until tomorrow."

"Crap."

"Excuse me?"

"I'm sorry." She sighed heavily. God, she might as well tell him. He'd probably figure it out anyway. "I really need someone with a four-wheel-drive vehicle to help me."

"I'm available."

Crap again. Not that she didn't want help; she just didn't want Cole's help. And for more reasons than one. She obviously had unresolved issues where Cole was concerned and now wasn't the time to deal with them.

"Did I say the wrong thing?"

She had to smile. "No. Can I come over?"

"Sure. Like I said, I'm available."

She told him she'd be there in fifteen minutes, then went to the café and made sure the Closed sign was on the door. She suspected her regular customers had already been there and gone, but too bad. This was more important. She made another couple of calls to Ryan's number, to no avail, then got back in her van and drove down the street.

COLE HAD BARELY PICKED up his steaming mug of coffee and lifted it to his lips, when the front door burst open and slammed against the wall with a thud.

"Sorry," Serena said, then pulled herself up and squared her shoulders. She wore jeans and a red, long-sleeved Cosmic Bean T-shirt, and when he saw the look on her face, he knew something was wrong. He set his cup down and circled the desk to her side.

She gazed at him with big wide eyes. "I need help." She swung around. "I know you'll probably say the same thing as Karl did, but I really need some understanding here."

He motioned for her to sit, then he sat on the corner of the desk, waiting for her to explain.

"Okay. Don't jump to conclusions and tell me that I'm doing what Ryan wants me to do. This is different. I know Ryan is in trouble."

He remembered she'd had similar feelings back in high school. Sometimes she'd been right, sometimes not.

"I'm pretty sure I know where he went, and I need someone with a four-wheel drive to go with me. I thought I could get Sam to do it, but he's not here. I'd pay you to go, just like a tour and—"

He raised a hand. "You think Ryan is lost? Or do you think something might've happened to him?"

"Either or both. I don't know. But my feelings tell me he's not in hiding to spite us. Karl won't go because he thinks Ryan is a screwup and he's done this before, and I really can't blame Karl for that. So please, will you help me?"

Man, she didn't need to go through all that. All she had to do was ask, period. After this week, he'd decided he'd go with the flow where Serena was concerned. Whatever that might be. "I have a one-hour tour at one o'clock, but I can go right after that. And there's no need to pay me. I'm happy to help."

"Really?" She appeared truly surprised, then said, "No, I have to pay you. You have to let me do that."

"Okay." He sipped his coffee. "Do you want to get some other people in town to help search?"

She shook her head. "Not yet. I'm pretty sure I know where he went, and if he's not there, then yes, that's a good idea."

"So, you know where to go?"

Nodding, she said, "There're a couple of

places to check. Not that long ago, he mentioned some mines we used to retreat to when things weren't going very well at home."

"When was that? You never mentioned—"

"Before you and I started seeing each other. The mines are in the Bradshaws. There's the Appaloosa Mine and the Old Buzzard Mine, and one other. Big Bart—that's it. They're all fairly close together."

"Yeah, but they must not be on any of the forest service maps or I would have checked them out for tours."

"Maybe not."

"And if they're not on the maps, the roads are probably really rough."

She frowned. "I realize that. Actually, you should check them out because sometimes the smaller ones have a richer history and would be good for some of your tours."

He smiled. "You're an excellent saleswoman. If you ever need a job, give me a call."

She tried to smile but her forehead furrowed instead, and that told him she was really worried.

"When do we leave?"

He shouldn't have made a joke. But she looked so cute and so sincere, and he'd just wanted to pull her into his arms and hug her.

"As soon as I'm done with the other tour. Let's say, two-thirty."

Her eyes got big again. She pursed her lips. "Thank you, Cole. I really appreciate it." And then she turned and left.

Cole drew in a big breath and watched her drive away. She really appreciated it. That might've made him feel good if he wasn't the reason Ryan had run off in the first place. After everyone had left the other day, Ryan had called Cole on his cell and told him they were going to get what they wanted: he'd not be around anymore to bother anyone again.

Cole hadn't taken the bait and simply said, fine. That it was about time Serena had a normal life. Ryan had gone totally quiet, didn't say another word, and then the phone had clicked in Cole's ear. Ever since, he'd wondered if what he'd said might've been the proverbial final straw for Ryan.

"THIS IS IT," SERENA SAID, eyeing the road before them. From what she could tell on the map, they were approximately halfway to the old Buzzard Mine. So far the road hadn't been too bad, but she could see where the paved road stopped ahead.

Cole pointed to a sign to their left: Ungraded Road. High-clearance Vehicles Only. Enter at Your Own Risk. "Hope it's not too bad," he said sympathetically. His smile cheered her. Up until this moment she'd been unsure if he planned to continue to help her. She'd thought he might give up and turn back.

Gravel crunched under the wide tires as they continued on. The road soon became an obstacle course, with deep ruts formed by water runoff from the mountains. Cole concentrated on maneuvering the vehicle around the debris and the occasional boulder that had fallen onto the road from above.

Jostled from side to side, Serena gripped the safety handles. Every muscle in her body tensed as she anticipated each jolt.

The vehicle lurched, and Serena flew upward, then slammed down into the seat. The loud crunch of metal against rock came from underneath and the vehicle thudded to a stop in a cloud of dust. They glanced at each other and then at the road in front of them.

"What the hell?" Cole said, still looking around. He stepped on the gas, but the vehicle didn't move.

"It felt like we hit something."

He didn't answer but threw the gearshift into Reverse and gave the engine some juice. Still nothing.

"Yeah." Cole cursed. He opened his door to get out, and Serena followed suit. Her door scraped on something and when she stepped down, the ground under her foot yielded. "Oh, crap." She grabbed the door and caught herself. Hoping to see what was going on, she edged away from the car. "Good grief. We're in a hole."

"No kidding." Cole pushed his hat to the back of his head and wiped the sweat from his brow with his forearm. He thought for a second, then stalked over to where she stood. "We're wedged in on one side." He pointed toward the back. "The seat extension kept us from dropping. If we'd been in a shorter vehicle, we'd have dropped deeper and been unable to get out." He gazed at her.

"That's creepy." She touched a hand to her throat. "It's probably one of those sinkholes where the water runs underground and eventually the soil above collapsed. I've heard of entire homes being swallowed up that way."

He continued to gaze at her.

"Really," she assured him. "There was a fissure like this under a major road in Scottsdale not that long ago. One day the asphalt simply split open and a couple of cars dropped in."

"Well, then we're fortunate it's only big enough for the tires." He glanced around at the craggy mountains surrounding them, then strode across the road in front of the car, stopped, gingerly kicked the ground, then straddled another rut. "Can you get that flashlight in the back?" he requested, and when she brought it, he got down on his knees and checked under the car.

"Can't see anything."

With the sun scorching her bare shoulders, Serena felt sweat run down the inside of her arms. Damn. She was probably sunburned already. She untied her shirt from around her waist, put it on and then pulled out her cell phone.

"Forget it. You won't get any reception with all the mountains around. Wait until we're in a clearing."

She tried the phone anyway, but discovered he was right. She pushed back her bangs and leaned against the driver's door. "So what now? Should we send up smoke signals?"

He grinned at her.

"What?" she asked.

He pointed to her head, so she glanced in the side mirror. Her hair was even frizzier than normal and her ponytail was lodged on the side of her head.

Cole smiled. "I can't believe you still look like a teenager." He reached out to touch her face.

She stepped back.

"Dirt," he said. "You've got dirt on your face."

He reached again, only this time she didn't move as he brushed his fingers across her cheek. In those few seconds, a host of memories flooded back. Her heart pounded crazily. "Uh… Okay. I think we'd better figure out how to get out of here."

An hour later, they stopped by a large boulder on the shady side of the mountain, energy sapped. They'd walked at least a mile farther down the road to see if they could spot any signs of life. But the road just went on and on, winding through the foothills.

Nothing had appeared familiar to Serena, and by the time they returned to the Jeep, it was late afternoon, and the temperature had peaked. They still had a few hours before sunset, but once the sun dropped below the mountain, it would be dark, and unless there was a full moon, nothing was darker than the desert at night. Cole, she was certain, wouldn't be foolish enough to travel these roads in the dead of night. They'd be stuck out here.

Cole sat down, leaned back, pushed his hat down over his face and said, "Might as well rest a minute."

She sat down, too, wrapped her arms around her legs and laid her head on her knees. During the ride, she'd wanted more than anything to ask Cole about the accident. When she'd visited him in jail, he'd had little memory of what happened before or right after the accident.

Mostly, she wanted to know why he'd stayed at the party. What was so compelling that he couldn't have said no? But every time she thought about asking, she realized how pointless it was.

No one could turn back the hands of time. And even if *she* could somehow manage to get beyond the accident, there was the baby. If she knew nothing else, she knew that Cole would never forgive her for keeping his son from him.

To even think in that direction was stupid.

But for just a few moments, she wanted to savor the fantasy.

Her gaze drifted to Cole again. His arms were crossed over his chest, one leg was stretched out and the other was bent at the knee. Just looking at him, his muscular body, the curve of his chin, his sensual mouth, brought memories of desperate young love and nights of exploratory passion.

She tore her eyes away and glanced at the mountains where spheroidal rocks like giant bowling balls balanced precariously one atop the other. One big wind and they could come tumbling down. A metaphor for her life right about now. She hadn't felt so unsettled since returning to Spirit Creek five years earlier. But everything would revert to normal once she found Ryan and went back home. It would. It had to.

As she sat there studying the rocks and

scrubby trees, an idea hit. She scrambled to her feet, ran back to the Jeep and pulled out the flashlight, then went to the front of the vehicle and peered at the tires on the side of the vehicle that was in the hole. *It just might work.*

Excited, she picked up a rock and tossed it into the hole behind the tire. Then she found a few more rocks and tossed them in.

"What the hell are you doing?"

She turned. Cole had walked up behind her. Smiling, she brushed at the hair hanging in her face with her forearm.

"I have an idea."

"Well, until I figure out a plan, you should be saving your energy."

She waved at the truck. "But I have an idea how to get us out."

His eyes widened skeptically. "An idea."

"Yes. We fill up the hole with rocks, find something flat to put under the tires, and drive out."

He scratched his head. "Something flat, huh?" He swiveled, squinting as he searched the landscape. "Where are we going to find something flat?"

Her gaze followed his. "Hmm. Good point." Her excitement faded just a bit. "Well, we've got to do something. Maybe if we start filling the hole, we'll think of a solution. At the very least, if we fill the hole, maybe we can push the Jeep out."

He blinked, his expression blank.

"Unless you have another idea."

After another long moment, he rubbed his chin again and said, "Rocks, huh? I guess the idea's worth a try."

She couldn't help smiling. "Well, let's get started then." She swept past him, climbing higher on the mountainside, and began rolling rocks toward him. "I'll roll—you chuck."

Night descended quickly, and when the hole was close to being filled, Cole said, "Even if we get the Jeep out, we'll have to stay put for the night and head back in the morning. These roads are rough enough even when you can see."

Bringing a shoulder up this time to wipe the sweat off her face, Serena nodded. "Okay. Whatever."

Cole watched Serena, admiring her stamina. Her hair hung in frizzy curls around her sunburned face, her body was covered with dust, her shirt was drenched with sweat, yet she looked adorable.

"Okay," she said. "I've got another idea."

He crossed his arms. "I'm all ears."

"See those paloverde trees? There are a lot of dead branches on the ground underneath."

He thumbed his hat back. "Yeah. What about 'em?"

"Now that the rocks are bracing the tires, we could bind some of those dead branches and stuff them under the tires to give us traction to get out."

Gazing at them, he said, "You know, that's a good idea. I have some rope and bungee cords in the back."

Together they collected the largest branches they could find, lined them up lengthwise, wove the rope through the strips and used a bungee cord to secure them. When they finished, the thing resembled a makeshift raft. If they'd been stranded on a desert island, they could've floated away.

Within the hour, they'd jacked the car up and wedged branches under the front and back tires to form a short bridge.

"Okay, it's now or never," Cole said, holding up crossed fingers. He opened the door and eased onto the seat, careful not to make any moves that might shift things around. He stuck the key into the ignition and switched on the engine.

The vehicle was hotter than an inferno, and sweat ran down his arms and even his legs. His hatband was soaked, as was his T-shirt. He offered up a small prayer to any deity who might want to smile on him, then he shifted into gear, rocked forward, shifted and rocked back, using the same motion he employed when stuck in the snow in Chicago.

A rock clunked underneath, and the truck shifted sideways. He stomped on the gas. The Jeep jerked forward, upward and sideways. He floored the accelerator until the truck lurched ahead to rest on flat ground.

Relief flooded him. Serena ran up, beaming. He got out, and without thinking, he picked her up and swung her around with him.

Her hair tickled his face as she hugged him back, her body hot and sweaty against his. When she raised her smiling face to his, he felt an urgent need to kiss her. So he did. Her mouth was more tender than he remembered, her body more voluptuous. Slowly, he slid his hand from her shoulder to the curve of her waist, pulling her closer as he let her inch down until her feet touched the ground.

The pressure created an erotic sensation that nearly undid him. He deepened the kiss, his tongue seeking the sweetness of her mouth, a mouth that he remembered so well. When her arms came up around his neck, he forgot everything. And when she melted into him—he couldn't tell if *his* heart was pounding like a jackhammer or hers.

Damn. He wanted her as he'd never wanted anyone. And she seemed to want him just as much. His breathing was ragged as he eased his lips from hers and brought his mouth to her ear.

He held her tight, not wanting to ever let go, but then he felt her push, just enough to break the embrace. Though reluctant, he set her away from him. "Sorry," he said. "I guess I got a little overexcited." He shoved a hand through his hair and cleared his throat, no clue what to say next.

"Right. I, um…I don't know how that happened, either."

He did. Because he realized right then that all these years he'd been lying to himself. He'd convinced himself he didn't care about her. Didn't care that she'd gone off and married someone else while he rotted in jail.

But he did care. More than he'd ever imagined.

"Yeah. Me, too," he said. "Funny what the heat can do to a person." He turned to get back into the Jeep. "We better decide what to do next."

Serena retreated a step, then walked to the passenger side. He stared straight ahead, but in his peripheral vision he saw her touch her lips with her fingers.

God, he felt like an idiot. One minute he wanted her and the next, he wanted to get as far away as possible.

When would he learn that what he wanted didn't matter to anyone but him?

CHAPTER THIRTEEN

SERENA GLANCED AT THE quickly shifting sky, which had gone from cobalt to twilight gray in the blink of an eye. On the horizon, layers of crimson, sky-blue pink and purple backlit the distant mountain ranges. They'd only traveled a short distance when Cole stopped the truck in the middle of the road, got out his flashlight, opened the map and laid it over the steering wheel.

"What're you looking for?"

Cole turned his gaze to the sky. "We can't go much farther before it gets totally dark, so I'm looking for an alternative to sleeping under the stars tonight."

"What do you have in mind?"

After taking off his hat, he glanced at her, then returned her eyes to the map. A lock of hair hung over his forehead, and he reminded her of the boy she used to know. Her heart warmed at the endearing image. *If only…*

The thought was ridiculous. He wasn't that boy, and she wasn't the girl she'd been, either. Too much had happened to ever repair. "Is there another choice?" she asked absently. All she could think of was the kiss. The way they'd come together so naturally, as if the past hadn't happened.

"Yes. Miner's Gulch. I've been there a couple of times, but approaching it from the other direction. There might be a way to reach it through this pass. The road has been closed for a long time, but we might be able to get through within an hour or so."

She leaned toward him, craning to see the map without making any physical contact. The place didn't look far, but distance didn't mean much when mountains were involved.

"What's the worst thing that can happen? We sleep here or somewhere in between. In the morning we'll continue to the mine."

"Okay, I'm game." Good thing tomorrow was Sunday and the café would be closed.

"Yeah, I need a phone to let my mother know, or she'll be worried." That said, he cranked the steering wheel to the right and took off down a tiny road.

The road ahead was no bumpier than the one they'd been on; in fact, some places were less rugged.

By the time the sun had disappeared, they'd rumbled into Miner's Gulch. "I was here once when I was a kid, and it looks the same now as it did then." A few lights were on at the general store, which she remembered was the original building from the gold-rush days.

"Twenty-five permanent residents. I did some research for a tour." He pulled up in front of the store.

The place was rustic—wood and adobe, with a tin roof—and she imagined it appeared exactly as it had at the turn of the century. They both got out and climbed the creaky wooden steps to go inside.

The interior was just as rustic as the outside, and jam-packed with books, T-shirts and souvenirs of every type. There was also snack food, a smattering of silver-and-turquoise jewelry, a cooler full of soda and another full of ice cream. A small bank of post-office slots flanked a desk with a sign on the front that read Post Office. And above her head a plethora of Old West antiques hung from the ceiling. A huge white dog padded silently around them as if watching them.

A bearded man who looked to be in his early fifties stood behind a glass case filled with jewelry and knickknacks. Smiling, Cole walked over and said something, and they shook hands.

When they'd finished talking, Cole waved her over. "This is Serena Matlock. She runs the Cosmic Bean in Spirit Creek."

Serena shook the man's hand.

"I'm Michael," he said.

"We were out looking for one of the old mines and got stuck in a hole," Cole said. "When we finally freed our vehicle, it was too late to head back, so we're hoping there's some-place in Miner's Gulch to stay."

"We get a lot of backpackers out here. So we renovated the old bunk room above the saloon across the street. That's all there is, but you're welcome to stay," Michael said. "No one else is there right now."

Cole looked at Serena. "Sounds good to me."

He motioned for Cole to accompany him, and they went into another room behind some curtains. Serena busied herself looking at the jewelry, and when Cole returned, he handed her a key. "We can eat at the saloon," he said.

"Is there a shower in this bunk room?"

"Go check it out if you want."

She glanced at the key in her hand, then, and back at Cole.

"I'll be up in a few minutes. Leave the door open for me."

Serena gulped. The two of them spending the night in the same room was like putting a steak in front of a hungry lion. At least from her perspective.

"The staircase is on the outside of the building," Cole said as she went out the door.

She walked across the street and found the rustic wooden stairs, and as she ascended, she heard faint music playing somewhere in the background. Other than that, the night was silent. There were no city sounds—no engines, airplanes, buses, highways or congestion. No nightclubs or theaters. Just the natural sounds of night—and the creak of each step as she tested it on her way up.

The small town was probably like Spirit Creek before people started moving back into the old homes built during the mining boom. She liked the feel of the place, the steadiness. Here, as in Spirit Creek, things stayed the same. People stayed the same. Despite their flaws, you always knew where you stood.

Moving back to Spirit Creek had given her a sense of security she'd never felt. But more important, she felt a sense of belonging. The town didn't offer much excitement, but that was a small price to pay for the emotional comforts that living there provided.

She opened the door and groped the wall for a light switch. When she hit it, a light that resembled an old lantern popped on in one corner.

The room was large, with six cots lining one wall. A wooden table and four chairs sat in the middle of the room, and a sagging couch squatted on the opposite wall.

She found the bathroom and was filled with immediate relief when she saw the shower, primitive as it was. Within seconds she'd undressed and gotten inside. The warm water felt like a healing balm washing over her whole body, and she stayed there long after she'd finished washing. She was lost in the soothing sensation when she heard Cole's voice.

"Yo! Anyone here?"

She shut off the faucet, wrapped a towel around her head and toweled her arms and face. As she came out, Cole shoved a bundle of things into her hands. "Here, pick something out. Some T-shirts and stuff. Nothing fancy, but they're clean. There's a toothbrush in the bag for you, too."

"Thanks," she said and, still wrapped in the towel, started sorting through the bag. She could feel his eyes on her and, oddly, she wondered if he'd think her body had changed much in the years since he'd seen her without clothing.

"I called my mother," Cole said. "I'll call Sam in the morning to make sure he's doing okay." Ambling over, he pulled off the dirty shirt he was wearing. Then he picked a black T-shirt from the pile and headed for the bathroom.

And as he walked away, she couldn't help watching the play of muscles in his back, his narrow waist. She'd touched those muscles when he'd kissed her, felt the hard sinew flex as he held her in his arms. He was the same person she'd known so many years ago, yet he wasn't. He was a man, instead of a boy. He wasn't a stranger, yet he was.

When she heard water running, a vision of Cole standing naked under the warm water flashed in her head—Cole soaping his body into a slippery lather…then lathering her naked body. As she let her imagination wander, her stomach tightened with desire. Oh, man. She stopped the fantasy, then quickly picked out a navy blue T-shirt and a pair of cargo pants, both of which advertised the Miner's Gulch General Store. She put them on but couldn't bring herself to don her sweaty underwear, which she could wash tonight and have fresh for morning.

Oh, yes. She felt so much better she hugged herself. She crossed the room to the window, opened it and breathed in the tangy scent of high-desert air, an earthy mixture of sage and mesquite. Standing there, she chastised herself for thinking about Cole when she should be worrying about Ryan.

She drew a long breath. What if Ryan showed up at home and she wasn't there? She chewed on her bottom lip, wondering if she'd made the right choice to go on her gut feeling. It had been the most compelling one she'd had. Otherwise she might be at home waiting by the phone for Ryan to call.

After dropping onto the chair next to the window, she towel-dried her hair, and then finger-combed it to let it air-dry. When she reflected, she knew why Ryan hadn't mentioned the loan from Bella. It would be one more time he'd disappointed her. Her brother might not be the most dependable person in the world, but she knew he felt worse than anyone when he messed up time after time. She couldn't give up on him. She could never give up on him, she realized. No matter what he did.

When Cole emerged from the shower, his hair was wet and combed straight back. His beard had gone more than a tad past the five-o'clock-shadow stage, making him appear more like an outlaw than Indiana Jones. But definitely the sexiest outlaw ever.

The black T-shirt molded to his chest, its short sleeves showing off his muscular biceps. What a dramatic contrast between him and her. When they walked down the stairs and into the saloon, she felt like a pair of birds, where the male was colorful and showy and the female drab and plain.

They went around the building to the entry. Above the door, Last Chance Saloon was printed in lopsided lettering. The place was empty except for a lone woman behind the bar.

"This is Serena Matlock," Cole said to the woman, who looked a little like Barbra Streisand. "And this is Margo, Michael's partner."

Margo smiled. "Nice to meet you."

"They practically run this town," Cole said as he led Serena toward a booth on the other side of the room. When they sat, Margo came over to take their orders. The menu was limited. Serena ordered a cheeseburger and fries, while Cole ordered a chicken chimichanga platter, and when Cole ordered a beer, Serena did, too.

Once Margo left, Cole studied Serena's face with interest. "I didn't think you liked beer."

"I didn't. But…people change."

After Margo brought two frosty beers and a couple of Mason jars, Cole reached over and poured beer down the inside of Serena's glass, then set it before her. He said, "That's right. People do change."

He leaned back in the booth, tipped his bottle to his lips and took a swig. His Adam's apple moved as he swallowed. His tongue slid across his moist lips.

"So, are you still in touch with Brett?"

Well, that had come out of nowhere. She lifted her glass and sipped, avoiding his penetrating gaze. "Nope." And she hoped that would be the end of that conversation.

Cole was quiet for a moment, continued to study her. "How long were you married?"

Her pulse jumped. "Not long. We knew right away it was a mistake. We stayed friends, but once he got married again, that pretty much ended, too. And after his mom died he never returned to Spirit Creek." She shrugged. "Sometimes you just have to put the past to rest." Just as she hoped he'd put this line of conversation to rest.

He picked at the label on his bottle of beer. "Maybe. But sometimes that's impossible to do it if issues haven't been resolved."

She knew exactly what he was alluding to. And maybe he was right. Maybe if they got it all out, she'd be able to forget it.

He moistened his lips again. "Why didn't you tell me the real reason you broke off with me?"

Her heart stopped. She couldn't breathe. He couldn't know, could he? "The real reason?"

His lips thinned as he wrapped both hands around the neck of the beer bottle; then his mouth quirked up on one side, as though he was trying to smile but couldn't. "Yeah. Why didn't you just tell me you were seeing someone else? If you had, I wouldn't have wasted my time writing all those letters. I wouldn't have kept waiting and hoping. I wouldn't have kept waiting for someone to bring me a letter, or tell me I had a visitor."

Oh, God. Was that what he'd thought? "I—I don't know where you got that information, but it's totally untrue. Why would you think that?"

He straightened. "Why wouldn't I? You got married practically before they locked my cell door."

She closed her eyes for a second, tried to calm the nerves rioting inside. "It wasn't soon." She quickly counted—she'd been nearly four months along when she last saw Cole, and she'd married Brett three months after giving birth. "It was eight months later, but the last time I saw you, I told you exactly how I felt." Her heart thumped so hard she couldn't stand it. "I told you it was over. But all that was years ago, Cole. We were kids who didn't know anything about anything. At least I didn't. And if I didn't handle everything just right, I'm sorry." She drew a breath. "We have to go on. I've made an effort to do that. But most important, it wasn't about you and me as much as it was about all the other stuff."

Cole looked as if he was about to say something, when Margo brought their food.

A dark silence hung between them, but then Cole said, "Sorry. You're right. Your marriage is none of my business." His eyes met hers, and he coughed to clear his throat. "Despite how everything ended, I hope he was good to you."

Seeing the hurt in Cole's eyes, she felt as if she'd betrayed him. And she hadn't. He'd been the one to do that. But she'd wasted enough time on all that. It was over. "He was. He was a good man."

Cole nodded, as if that somehow closed the book on the past. They ate dinner in near silence. Cole finished first, then sat quietly observing her while she finished her meal. For some reason, she started to feel more relaxed, as if they'd reached an understanding. She sensed he felt the same. It was almost as though getting out all the hard feelings had freed them to be normal again.

After Serena was done, Cole asked Margo if they could put the meal on the tab for the room, and then they went upstairs.

"Not bad for a bunk room that held forty to fifty miners at a crack, is it?" Cole said. "Go ahead. Take your pick."

Serena immediately went to the bunk farthest

from Cole and she suddenly felt exhaustion creeping through every muscle in her body. "Do you need to use the bathroom?" she asked. "I might be a while."

"I'll wait," Cole said, then went to the bed nearest the window.

When Serena had finished, Cole did likewise, then went directly to bed. Three hours later, she was still awake. The room was too warm, and she had to kick off her covers. Even though she was more physically and emotionally exhausted than she'd been in a long time, her mind continued to spin. That she could see him outlined in shadow from the moonlight slanting through the front window didn't help. He slept bare chested atop the blanket, in a pair of souvenir jogging shorts like hers, and though his eyes were shut, she wondered if he was really asleep.

She thrashed around on the bed, rearranging the sheet so her feet stuck out but the rest of her was covered. A wooden fan clacked rhythmically overhead, but even so, she could hear Cole's every breath, and the rustle of his sheet when he moved even the slightest.

"Better get some sleep," he said softly.

When she heard his deep, sleepy voice, her heart did a *ka-thump.* She waited a moment then said, "I'm too worried to sleep." She waited another moment, then added, “How come you’re awake?”

“I’m wondering what it would be like to kiss you again.”

Longing filled her once more. How many times had she thought about kissing him? How many times had she thought about making love with him again? “You’re right,” she said. “We both should get some sleep.”

A half hour later, she got up, walked across the room and slipped into bed next to Cole. He took her into his arms.

“Hi,” he said softly.

“Hi.”

He linked his fingers with hers and rubbed his thumb down her arm.

“I’ve thought about you so many times over the years,” he said. “Thought about the accident and what I should have done so things wouldn’t have ended the way they did. But I’ve never been able to come up with anything.”

“Shh.” She placed a finger over his lips. “I’ve thought about you, too.” More than she wanted to admit. Even to herself.

The moment their lips met, Serena knew exactly what Cole had meant when he’d said they had unfinished business. He was referring to the need to put finality to years of indecision about where they stood with each other. Sex might not be the answer, but yearning for the closeness they'd once shared, she was more than willing to find out.

She savored the taste of his mouth, the silky texture of his skin just inside his bottom lip. She reveled in his touch, his fingers moving slowly, teasing every sensitive nerve in her body. His touch as a teenager had been tentative and urgent, as opposed to sure and slow, which it was now. Everything was the same...yet nothing was the same at all.

When he stroked her stomach, she remembered the child she'd carried. His child. And for one crazy moment, she thought it could happen again. Maybe there was a chance for them, a chance to live the life that had been snatched away. The possibility brought reality to the fore. "Cole," she whispered.

"Uh-huh." His lips kept moving down her neck to her breasts and her stomach.

She could barely get out the words. "Protection."

He stopped, but just for a second. "We're covered," he said, then reached down for his backpack. "I grabbed Sam's backpack by mistake, and guess what I found in it." He rustled around a bit and brought up a silver packet.

"Thank you, Sam," she said. Then took the packet from Cole's hand and ripped it open.

"No, wait. I'm not ready for that." He nuzzled her neck.

"I beg to differ. You're more than ready."

"But you aren't. I want to make you scream."

She laughed. "You haven't changed." She slid the packet under the pillow and climbed on top of him. "And I haven't, either."

COLE WAS IN SERIOUS trouble. He shouldn't be here, lying in bed ready to make love with a woman who had the ability to shred his heart. But he couldn't think of anyplace he'd rather be. Shredded heart or not. And when he looked into those tawny eyes, searching for something that said she felt the same as he did, something that told him he wouldn't regret this for the rest of his life, she answered him with her lips.

Her skin was soft and damp, warm and sleek, and the little sounds low in her throat urged him on. He kissed her neck and the tender spot at the base of her throat while he ran his hands over her perfect little breasts and the curve of her smooth narrow hips. He reached up and slipped off the T-shirt she was wearing and pulled back to look at her—so perfect in the moonlight. He leaned forward and brushed his lips across the creamy smoothness of her breasts, trailing his tongue to the very tips of her baby-pink nipples.

She gasped, then ran her fingers over the muscles in his back, as if feeling every sinew, and suddenly their hands were flying, as though in a hurry to touch each and every inch of skin before the moment could get away. With her naked body pressed against his, he couldn't think of anything except getting as close to her, in every way, as he could.

They tumbled around, caught in a whirlwind of sensation. Every place she touched him burned with desire, and every place he touched her made him want her even more.

Then he realized that he didn't just want her—he needed her. Needed her in a way he'd never needed anyone.

She pulled him closer and wrapped her legs around him as though urging him to hurry and get on with it. But he didn't want that. He wanted to go on forever; he wanted to bring her to the brink, hear her call his name. He wanted her to want him as much as he wanted her.

Her face glowed in the moonlight and, looking at her, he realized that from the moment he'd returned to Spirit Creek and seen her outside the café, he'd known this moment was as inevitable as the sunrise. He pulled her closer still, nuzzling her neck and her ear, kissing her eyes and her nose and her chin and everything he could before their lips met once again.

She snuggled against him, quietly touching and teasing, her hips moving rhythmically against him, her tongue tracing a hot path around the circle of his ear. Then she laughed, a throaty sexy laugh, as she brought one hand down to touch him…and nearly sent him over the edge. Somehow they managed to get out the packet and in the next instant he was inside her. She was firebrand-hot and slick with desire. He covered her mouth with his in a long, deep and sensuous kiss, his tongue keeping the same rhythm as their bodies.

He thrust slowly at first, not wanting to hurt her in any way, yet wanting with all his heart to make it as wonderful for her as he possibly could. But she raised her hips to him, moving faster and faster, and the pressure inside him continued to build until he thought he'd burst.

But he wasn't about to let go before— All of a sudden, she moaned with an urgency he recognized, and he let himself go, giving himself up to the hot physical sensations that exploded inside him, satisfied in knowing she'd been there with him every step of the way.

CHAPTER FOURTEEN

SERENA AWAKENED TO find Cole gone, and for one fraction of a second, panic seized her, the same horrible feeling she'd had as a little girl when her parents disappeared. But then, a slow smile emerged as she remembered last night—the most amazing, incredible night ever.

She stretched out and closed her eyes again, imagining the tender, loving way Cole had run his fingers across her bare shoulders and down her spine, gently stopping along each vertebra. He'd learned a lot since they were teenagers experimenting with an all-consuming passion. Cole's sureness and certainty excited her in ways she couldn't have imagined. Instead of teenage infatuation and lust, she'd been emotionally and physically engaged, body and soul.

But as much as she wanted to stay in bed and dream about Cole, she couldn't. She had to find Ryan before he got himself in even worse trouble. The thought of Ryan tamped down her optimism. To consider the lovemaking anything more than an interlude was presumptuous. Most likely, Cole hadn't thought twice about it. They'd had unfinished business, he'd said. So now they were done. Finished. And her only concern had to be finding her brother.

She rolled out of bed and padded into the bathroom. First thing on her agenda this morning was getting to a phone. She wanted to call the condo on the off chance Ryan had gone home, and she wanted to call Lucy to see if she'd heard any more. If she couldn't find Ryan, she'd have to call Karl, even though she doubted the sheriff would do much of anything.

Once done washing her face, she brushed her teeth and stuck the toothbrush in the glass next to Cole's. A wistful, nostalgic feeling flowed over her. If the accident had never happened, they'd be an old married couple, and have shared the same bathroom for years.

After digging in her tote bag, she pulled out Ryan's baseball cap and glanced at her image in the mirror. What a pitiful mess she was. Her arms now had a farmer's tan, her hair looked like a haystack and her freckles seemed even more pronounced after being in the sun all day yesterday. She bunched her frizzy hair into a ponytail and shoved it through the hole at the back of the baseball cap, then settled the visor low on her forehead to protect her face from the sun.

COLE SAID GOODBYE, and as he reset the receiver, he saw Serena hurrying across the street toward the general store. He stepped out of Michael's office, a tiny room next to the post-office boxes on one wall. He'd talked to Sam, who was doing two tours today. His mom was fine and everything was under control. He could continue to help Serena hunt for Ryan and not worry about other stuff.

He owed her that. He owed Ryan.

Serena entered the store and immediately came over to where Cole was standing.

"Ready for some breakfast?" he asked.

"Sure," she said. "But I need to make a few phone calls first."

"I made my calls already." Cole stepped aside, giving her access to the phone. The room was a tangle of throw rugs, pillows, videotapes, magazines, newspapers, computer materials and CDs. An eclectic assortment of books lined one wall, and another wall sported an old maple console television with a round-cornered screen.

Cole stood at the counter to talk to Michael, but he saw Serena dial a number on the old rotary phone, listen and then hang up. She dialed another and he saw her talking to someone.

He didn't know what to think about last night, but he sure felt great. He'd thought about making love with her so many times since returning to Spirit Creek that he practically had every movement memorized. But he'd never believed it would happen. That she was as eager as he was made it even more sensational. But that was as far as he was going to go with it. She'd given him no indication that their lovemaking had been anything more than a one-night stand. And unless she told him otherwise, he'd leave it at that. He'd help her find Ryan, and when he had the company back in the black, he'd do whatever he could to convince Ryan to sell it and get on with his life.

When Serena was done with her calls, Cole handed her the sack of food Margo had made for them. "Breakfast," he said. "Since it's getting late, I thought it would be faster to eat on the road."

She looked at the container. "Smells good."

"It's something like a McDonald's Egg McMuffin. I have a thermos full of coffee and some covered cups, too."

"Great. I'm all set whenever you are."

Just then Margo came in. "Well," she said, "I see you're ready to depart."

"We are," Cole said, then thanked both Margo and Michael for their hospitality and told them that if they got to Spirit Creek, to stop by the touring company. Serena chimed in with her invitation to visit the café.

"Cole," Serena said once they reached the Jeep, "just so you know, last night was great, but it was a one-time thing. We're both adults and smart enough to realize it can never be anything other than that."

He poked around the truck, checking the tires, the fenders, then slipped into the driver's seat and cranked the engine. Grateful he was wearing sunglasses so she couldn't see his eyes, he looked at her and shrugged. "I never thought anything else."

He motioned for her to climb into the passenger side. "If we don't get going, it'll be too damn hot to do anything."

The look on her face as she slipped into the passenger seat was priceless. Almost as though she expected him to object to her pronouncement.

He watched her adjust the mister without turning it on. She was wearing the same T-shirt she'd picked out last night, but like him, she had her jeans on again.

And she was wearing white bikini underwear.

The thought made his blood rush. Ever since he'd gone into the bathroom this morning and seen the slip of fabric dangling on the towel rack to dry, he'd had more than one fantasy. He'd imagined tucking his hand behind the front band and inching his fingers down her silky skin, feeling her move against him the way she had last night.

He wondered how that stark white underwear would look against the vee where her thighs met, remembered her firm calves wrapped around him. And for just a moment, he was transported to the past, to a time when all he'd wanted was to marry Serena and raise a family with her. A real family, with a mom and a dad and kids who were confident in their parents' love.

At the click of a seat belt snapping into place, he came to attention.

"Ready?" Serena asked.

He sighed, wistful. "Ready as I'll ever be."

Within the hour they were back on the road, at the spot where they'd been stuck in the hole, but now they were driving in the other direction, farther into the Bradshaw Mountains.

He drove cautiously, his eyes alternately watching the road then the mountains for signs of loose boulders that might tumble down on them.

The next few miles to the turnoff seemed to take forever. And when they reached it, it looked more like an overgrown hiking trail, with hidden gullies and potholes. Next to it was a wash filled with sand, rocks and debris.

"This looks like a better course," Cole said as he cranked the wheel and plunged them into the wash.

"Wait," Serena yelled, clutching the door handle for dear life. "You can't drive in a wash," she sputtered, her words rattling like her bones as the truck bounced over rock after rock.

Cole turned to her with a smirk. "I can't?"

Serena bristled. "It's dangerous. There could be a flash flood." She'd seen more than one flash flood on the news—a massive wall of water hurtling forward with more force than a freight train. A force that moved boulders and uprooted trees.

He glanced to the sky. "And it doesn't look like rain. But we don't have far to go, do we?" His voice had gone softer. "At least, not according to calculations."

"We should be getting close. But nothing looks familiar."

Cole jammed his foot on the brake.

"I'm sure it's right around here," she said. "It's just…there are so many small hills, so many—"

Before she finished her sentence, he'd shut off the engine, opened the door and jumped from the driver's seat. He stalked toward the front of the vehicle and yanked open the hood.

"What's wrong?" She stood and peered over the windshield.

"Nothing, I hope. The gauge spiked, so I wanted to check it out."

"And?"

"I have to let the engine block cool off to look. But I think we're okay. Nothing's leaking, anyway."

While Cole checked under the hood again, Serena scanned the area, trying to get her bearings. They were close; she felt it.

Then she caught sight of a dark shape in the distance. "Oh…there!" She pointed, even though he wasn't looking. "I think I see it!"

Cole raised his head.

"There, over the top of that foothi—"

"Oh, man! Dammit!" Cole kicked the tire.

"What?"

"We're leaking like a sieve."

"Can you fix it?"

"I don't know." He sighed. Placed his hands on his hips. "Did you say something else?"

"Yes." She pointed again. "Over there. I think that's the old miners' shack that's not too far from the mine."

"That's great. Only, now we can't get there."

He glanced down at the engine. "Toss me the duct tape that's in the back, will ya?"

She twisted around and rummaged through the box of supplies behind her, found the tape and handed it to him. A gust of hot, dry wind blew sand in her face.

Cole continued to do something under the hood; then, when finished, he came around, took the last plastic container full of water, poured some into their two small bottles and emptied the rest into the radiator.

Soon they were on the road again, but the shack really was farther than it looked. They'd gone up and down so many moguls that she'd lost sight of the building and hoped to hell they hadn't gotten off course.

Continually searching the area as they drove on, Serena saw ahead an overgrown sand road that she was certain led to the actual mine.

"I think we can get there using that road off to the left," she said. "It goes right by that old miners' camp."

They slowed to a near stop. "But where's the mine?"

She pointed ahead. "About halfway up and around the left side of that mountain. You can't make it out from here. It's so strange that I didn't remember it being so far."

"I don't see any evidence anyone has come this way. Do you?"

She shook her head and looked away, but not before he noticed the disappointment in her eyes.

"No, but it's possible Ryan could've gone to the mine from the other direction. And even if he's not there, I'll know and won't have to wonder about it."

Understandable. If he were her, he'd want to know, too. They spent another fifteen minutes bumping along the poor excuse for a road before they reached the shack. It was about the size of a small one-car garage, the wood was rotted, the tin roof was missing on one side and boards were nailed like a cross over the front door and over the two small windows on either side.

"Let's stop and check around," Cole said. "Find out if anyone has been here."

"Cole. Look." She pointed to her left. "I spotted something over there."

Following her hand, Cole spotted it, too, some kind of metal container, but he couldn't tell exactly what it was. "Yeah. But the terrain's too rugged to drive that way. I'll walk over."

He took off, and then Serena remembered the small oasis a little farther beyond the shack. They needed water. Any water was better than none.

She grabbed the two plastic water containers and started to follow him. "Cole," she called out.

He stopped. "What's wrong?" Cole was beside her in an instant. "What are those for?"

"There's a water hole beyond the shack. We should fill these up just in case."

"Okay. Let's go."

It was quiet, really quiet. All she could hear was the crunch of hard sand underfoot and the occasional flutter of a lizard or a roadrunner scurrying nearby.

Coyotes and mountain lions roamed the hills. Wolves, too. But she didn't want to let her thoughts roam in that direction. Then something rustled in the brush to her left and she jerked around to see. Her heart thudded wildly in her chest.

Cole caught her. "Hey. What's wrong?"

"I thought I heard something." She looked around. "But obviously I was wrong. I guess I'm just anxious about Ryan."

He gave her a quick squeeze. "You're safe with me. I've got protection."

"Really. Always prepared?" She laughed, and a second passed before he got it, then he laughed, too. "Not that kind," he said. "Another kind."

Her eyes widened.

He pulled out a gun, then seeing the look on her face, he said, "On a tour, you never know."

She shook her head. “I always thought snakes and other desert animals are usually more afraid of us than we are of them. They don’t attack unless frightened or threatened.”

“I know. It’s the other kind of animal I worry about. The kind who smuggle people and drugs.”

She remembered what Karl had said. Cole could be more right than he knew. That was when she realized how little she really knew about him. She’d known the boy, not the man. And now she was intrigued. Wanted to know more. Wanted to know everything.

They found the water hole and filled the two containers, then went back to the car and drove toward the mine until the road petered out and he stopped. “I don’t see any tire tracks or anything. There’s no sign anywhere that indicates someone has been here. I think we should turn back.”

“No, we can’t. I have to be sure.”

“But we can’t drive any farther.”

She eyed Cole—defiantly, he decided.

“There’s a road over there.” She pointed to her left.

“If that’s a road, I’m Joan of Arc.”

She raised her chin and popped open her door. “Well, I’m going to the mine, even if I have to walk there.” She jumped from the car and started walking, her ponytail bouncing behind her.

He sat there, speechless, for a moment and watched her clomp off. A second later, he jerked the gearshift into Drive, pulled forward and leaned out the window. "Come back here. You can't walk."

She raised her head and he knew she'd heard him. And though he couldn't see her expression, he had a pretty damn good idea what it was. "Ah, for crissake!" He kept going until he reached her. "Will you please get in?"

She stopped and turned to him, the rising sun backlighting her hair, so that it resembled spun gold.

"This is ridiculous," Cole stated, stopping a little ahead of her and letting the engine idle.

"We can send the police back," he said.

"I already called Karl this morning and left a message where we are. But who knows if he's coming or not, and if we wait, it could be too late. We're here. We might as well finish what we started." She whirled again and forged onward, her boots kicking up angry dust clouds that mimicked her attitude.

The transmission grated as he jerked the Jeep in and out of gear. "C'mon, Serena. Be reasonable."

No response.

"Hey, talk to me. I'll go, but we have to have some rules." The vehicle bounced over a rock in the road and Cole lurched to the side. He grabbed the wheel to avoid being thrown out. He cursed. "If we get there and find nothing, will you promise to go back with me immediately?"

He saw her straighten. She stopped, turned and, with her feet planted squarely apart, squinted at him.

"I'm not going to leave you alone in the desert, so you might as well get in. You're my responsibility. I brought you out here and I have to take you back." He gave a quick nod. "C'mon. I'll drive you there, but you have to promise to come back immediately afterward."

She waited. "Okay. It's a deal."

THE MINE WAS AROUND the next bend, Serena was sure of it. But she'd stopped saying anything just in case it wasn't. She held on to the door handle as the Jeep bounced up and down and side to side, from one rut to another, leaving a mushroom cloud of red dust in its wake. It was a wonder it held together at all under such punishment.

"It's right around the side of the mountain," Cole said. "You just didn't say which mountain." He raised his voice to be heard over the clunk and clank of rock against rubber and metal.

A thread of doubt unraveled her confidence.

She rubbed her sweaty palms on the legs of her jeans. The temperature had been a lot cooler when they'd started out, but now the day was getting hotter by the minute.

She felt a new layer of grit forming on her face and arms. Cole's hat was settled forward on his head and silver mirrored sunglasses shielded his eyes. His bronzed, muscular arms were raised, and he gripped the wheel with strong, capable hands.

Just then, as they rounded the curve, she spotted it.

"That's it! The Old Buzzard Mine!" Her pulse went ballistic. She was so excited she whacked him on the arm. "See!"

He put his finger to his mouth to shush her.

"I told you we'd find it soon," she whispered.

She unhooked her seat belt and rose up. About a quarter mile away, she could make out the shaft entrance a little above the foothills before them. After shifting in the seat to fasten her seat belt again, she glanced around for her hat. It was gone.

"That's it," she said, lifting her hand to indicate the direction of the mine. "Let's get a move on."

Cole reached down and pulled a pair of binoculars from the compartment between them. "Doesn't look like much to me. But we better be careful, anyway. Let's stop and figure out our next step."

"What's to figure out? If he's there, he's there. If not, he's not." That was the only part that worried her.

"Sorry. I know you're eager to find Ryan. In your place I would be, too. I just don't want to get any surprises."

She stared straight ahead. "It's okay."

"No, it's not. I know how much you care about Ryan. When you've picked up the pieces for someone all your life, it's tough to stop."

Serena glanced at Cole. He didn't have the whole story. No one did. And everyone always assumed she was doing too much.

"I see Keep Out signs, and boards sealing off the mine," Cole said, handing Serena the binoculars.

Serena took the glasses. "I'm not surprised. Although with the road essentially gone, who'd come out here to worry about?"

Cole glanced at Serena and tipped a wry smile. "People like Ryan, apparently."

Serena smiled back. "Right."

"It doesn't look like we can just drive right up, though."

They drove a little farther, ascending the foothills until they had to stop dead when the rock jutted upward in front of them. Cole cut the engine and exited the Jeep.

"That's it. We've got to hoof it from here."

As she was getting out, he went around to the back and pulled out a canvas bag before he bent down. In a second, he popped back up and, after shutting the door, he walked around to her side.

"Okay. Let's hit it!"

They couldn't see the mine shaft from where they stood, and Serena knew it wasn't as close as it seemed. As she'd reminded herself earlier, nothing in the desert was ever as close as it seemed.

"I'm as ready as you are."

Cole arched an eyebrow. Yeah, she was ready, all right.

CHAPTER FIFTEEN

CLIMBING UP A SMALL BANK, Cole offered Serena his hand, then steadied her as she picked her way across the rocky terrain. Her legs were unsteady, yet she never wavered, never complained.

When they finally arrived at the mine, he said, "Doesn't seem that anyone's been here in years." In fact, if the Keep Out signs hadn't been there, they might not have even found the place.

Serena picked her way toward the shaft entrance, where weathered boards crisscrossed a small opening in the side of the mountain. Cole grabbed her arm. "Don't get too close." The dangers around old mines were the unexpected—rock slides, sinkholes, snakes.

"It's okay. I've been in there before. Look—" She pointed to the top board. "The planks are barely attached. Almost as though someone was here recently. And look there." She whirled around. "Footprints."

Cole glanced at the gravel where she

pointed. "Animals. And I still think it's too dangerous to go any farther."

"Maybe for you, but I'm going to see if this—" She stepped forward and touched one of the old boards. On contact it shifted and fell off, clattering to her feet. "Ack!" She jumped back, and he caught her in his arms.

"It's okay," she said. "It startled me, that's all."

He considered holding her so she wouldn't pull any more stunts like that, but she felt too damn good and he couldn't trust himself. Reluctantly, he released his hold. She moved nearer the entrance and, using the fallen board, pried at the one remaining. His stomach knotted. She'd not be satisfied until she was one hundred percent sure her brother wasn't inside or hadn't been there. And she didn't care if she got hurt in the process.

But he did. No way was he gonna let anything happen to her.

"Here, let me do it." He muscled the board away.

"Great. I'm going in," she said.

"The hell you are."

Serena turned, then laughed him off. "It's safe. I've been in there before. This door leads to a cavern and the actual shaft goes down from inside." Her eyes narrowed slightly as she gazed at him. "Are you coming with me?"

Cole ground his back teeth and stifled his reservations. He lurched forward and motioned for her to follow him, placing a finger over his lips. "Shh," he whispered. "Just in case."

The mine was dark except for the faint light coming from the entrance. As his eyes adjusted, he inched forward, appreciating the fact that the farther they went, the cooler it got. As yet, he didn't need the flashlight he'd wedged into his back pocket.

So far, no sign of her brother. She closed her eyes. She felt him…and he was close.

A creature fluttered above them, and Serena scurried up behind him, grabbed on to the back of his shirt and huddled against him.

A few feet farther, they entered the inner sanctum. There was still enough light to see, and Serena quickly scanned for any sign of life. Cole inspected the center area, where the shaft was loosely covered by boards. Surrounding the shaft was a rail, and to the side of it, a rusty iron wheel and harness—apparently, the method used to haul ore up and down. Oddly, the place was clean, almost as if someone had been there recently and swept it out.

"Stay where you are," Cole instructed, holding up a hand while he checked the ground beneath their feet with a board he'd picked up at the entrance.

Serena halted. She waved toward another tunnel—a draft, as the miners called them. He knew the drafts led to smaller tunnels that fanned out into the mountainside in the quest for larger veins of gold or silver.

"Cole," Serena said.

"Keep it down," he whispered.

"But see, there's a tunnel. We need to take a look inside."

Cole ducked his head to flash a beam of light inside. "Too dark in there to see anything. Besides, there's no sign anyone was here. No tire tracks below, nothing inside."

"Ryan's been here. I feel him and he's in trouble. C'mon," she urged. "Let's go."

He didn't want to go, but he knew what it meant to her.

He grabbed her hand and pushed her ahead of him, his hands clamped around her waist. "Okay, let's go. But I want you right where I can see you."

Cole practically propelled Serena toward the exit. He dreaded going back into the heat after the small reprieve. As he followed her out, the glare of the sun almost knocked him to his knees, and he raised a hand to shield his eyes. Serena did the same. Then she positioned herself, feet apart, right hand shielding her eyes as she scanned the area.

She had to be disheartened over not finding her brother, but she had to know they couldn't remain out there forever. "C'mon. We'll go back home and and if Ryan hasn't returned, we'll get a search party. Maybe Natalia—"

A crack rang out, then something zinged off the rock beside him. He latched on to Serena and dived for cover. *What the hell!*

"Stay down," he ordered, dragging Serena farther behind the rock. Her eyes looked like moons; blood ran down her arm. His heart stumbled. Fearing she'd been shot, he bent to examine the wound, and was thankful to find just a bad scrape.

He ripped off his neck scarf. "Here. Wrap that on your arm and get behind me, over there." He indicated the boulder to the left of the shaft entrance. "And keep low!"

"Wh-what's going on?" Serena said, obviously shaken and confused.

"Someone's using us for target practice, so get down and stay down!" He pulled his pistol from his ankle holster.

Serena looked aghast—whether from surprise that Cole pulled his gun or horror that someone was taking potshots, he didn't know. Nor did he care. Following his orders, she crawled on her hands and knees to hide behind the rock.

"Just stay there. I've got to assess our position."

"Someone is shooting at us?" Serena asked incredulously.

"You got it." He picked up a large chunk of stone and tossed it out on the opposite side.

Zing, zing, zing. A barrage of gunfire ricocheted around them.

Squatting, he went to where Serena was huddled, arms wrapped around her knees, eyes locked on the weapon in his hand.

"It's okay. It's legal," he said in an awkward attempt to ease her fear.

Her hand went to her throat. "Wh-why would anyone—"

"Your guess is as good as mine," he answered before she'd finished.

"And what's that?"

"I think we interrupted someone doing something illegal."

Immediately, he thought of what the sheriff had told him several weeks ago about the FBI working on a huge bust in the area. "Maybe it's someone who believes we're claim jumpers."

Cole wondered if she'd intended that as a joke. But from the fearful look on her face, he could tell she was serious.

"People still work the mines. Eccentric people who could feel we're after something. When they learn they're mistaken and we're not going to do anything, it'll be okay."

Possibly. But he doubted it. "I bet it's someone doing something illegal. Like drug trafficking, or coyotes hauling a truckload of illegal immigrants." Those were the only likely possibilities for Cole. And he and Serena were sitting ducks.

He checked the cartridge, and in the instant his eyes were directed down, Serena was waving something white in her hand.

"Please stop shooting," she shouted. "We're only searching for someone who disappeared while hik—" *Zing, zing, zing.*

Cole shoved Serena down and blocked her with his body, letting loose a barrage of his own gunfire. He crooked an arm around her waist and dragged her like a rag doll back behind the rock. "Damn stupid thing to do," he hissed through his teeth.

For one god-awful moment he'd thought he'd lost her.

"Are you okay?" he asked on the next heavy breath.

She gave a tiny jerk of her head.

"Dammit. You gotta listen to me. These guys are serious. And it's not because we jumped their claim."

She glanced fearfully at his gun. "Why do you have that thing?"

"I always take a gun with me when I go out

in the desert. It's a safety precaution. And I've had lots of gun training."

He panned the area for an escape route of some kind. "You got any ideas on how to get out of here?"

She straightened. "There's the mine."

"Not on your life."

"It's safe. We could spot anyone coming in."

"It's a trap—the mine is a trap. We'd be sitting targets with no way out." He glanced right, left, up, down.

"There's another entrance to the mine on the west side, and a shaft that leads out near the base of the mountain." Her forehead furrowed. "I think."

"Can you get us there?"

Serena raised her chin. "I'm pretty sure."

"We've got shooters out there. Time is critical. Just tell me which way to go."

She glared at him and motioned for him to follow. When they'd eased their way around a few boulders and were, hopefully, out of sight of the shooters, Serena pointed to the right.

"Beyond that craggy corner is the entrance. It leads out farther down on the other side. The only problem is that when we exit, we'll be really far from the Jeep." She crossed her arms.

"Fine. Let's move it," Cole said, grasping her

hand. "We'll be out of range of the shooters. That's the important thing."

Serena had no time to reflect as they scrambled over the rocks and around the cactus, getting poked and scraped by every sharp thing in their path. But her physical discomfort was minuscule compared with her emotional turmoil. If Ryan was out here, he could have encountered these same men and who knows what might've happened. Now she was more certain than ever that her feelings had been right, though it was no consolation.

She avoided the woody spine of a dead cactus, and at the same time Cole caught her, his hold firm and decisive.

"How are you doing?"

"I'm fine. Just fine." They continued on, hunched down behind the larger rocks as they moved toward the west entrance to the mine. Cole shadowed her steps. When voices suddenly echoed from the other side of a large outcrop, he yanked her back and put his arms around her, as if to keep her still.

Apparently someone else knew about the other mine entrance. Good grief. Were these people together? How many were there? Were they surrounded on all sides?

Serena heard a man's voice from the other side of the boulder. "You stay and guard the hostage. We'll fan out and find who's out there."

Oh, God. Hostage?

"We can't have any witnesses," he said. "Shoot to kill. No one will ever find them out here."

Serena's heart stalled. Shoot to kill? Oh, God. Serena gasped.

Cole held her tighter, murmured "Shh" in her ear. Then he poised himself in front of her, obviously intent on protecting her. And he seemed to know what he was doing.

"Stay down. A couple of them are leaving," Cole whispered over his shoulder. He waited briefly, turned and flattened his back against the boulder next to her. His eyes narrowed, and he studied her. "You okay?"

She nodded. But she worried about Cole. His chest was heaving. The air was hot and dry, and sweat formed damp circles on his shirt under his arms, and lines across his shirt over his stomach. He'd lost his hat, too.

As she gazed at Cole, his every muscle appeared to ready for action. Despite the way Ryan had treated him, he was doing this for her brother. Or for her. Maybe both.

A bitter pill of remorse lodged in her windpipe. Their lives were at stake. She'd put Cole's life in danger and she was focused on herself.

She tried not to think that Ryan might be the hostage, but the thought kept coming back. And if Ryan was indeed a captive, she was to blame for trying to get him to do something he wasn't ready to do. Now she watched as Cole crept forward around the jagged outcrop, then stopped at a point where, apparently, he could see the other entrance to the mine.

"There're three," he said in a hushed tone. "We'll wait till two leave, then I'll take it from there." He crouched in position, maintaining vigil.

"What will you do?" she asked, her voice lowered to a near whisper.

He shot her a sharp glance. His eyes held no emotion, only hard purpose. "I'll do whatever I have to do to keep us safe."

She began to rise to get a look over his shoulder, but he stayed her with a hand to her arm.

"I'll wait until the two guards leave to look for us, then overtake the remaining guard."

Serena sucked in a shaky breath. "What should I do while you're doing that?"

"You'll stay right here where you're safe. When I'm done, I'll come back for you. I *will* get you out of here. That's a promise."

Serena jerked her head up. "I'm the one who got us into this mess. I should be helping."

His eyes softened as his gaze held hers.

"You didn't get me into anything. I made the choice to come."

She skimmed the contours of his face, the lines of purpose on either side of his mouth, the hard set of his jaw, and she realized the truth of it.

He could easily have taken her back. He could've taken her back at any time. But he hadn't. He'd come with her to find her brother. Whether for her sake or Ryan's, she didn't know. The fact was, he was here. A pang of guilt pierced her. He was a man willing to risk his life for others, and all she'd remembered was one thing.

"Okay. But if you're going to overtake that guard, I'm going to help."

Cole glared at her as though he knew she couldn't accept no for an answer. "Okay, but you have to do exactly as I say."

Serena nodded and peered through the fissure in the rock. Three guards stood hunched, studying something that appeared to be a map spread out on a rock. She couldn't see their faces, but the familiar stance of one man gripped her heart like an icy hand. It was the guy with the weird hair who'd been at Ryan's apartment. She didn't recognize the other guy. No question about it.

Then she heard their voices. "Okay, Wheeler, you head in that direction and I'll head the other way."

Cole took another look. "Okay, they've left, but now the other guard isn't there. He must've gone inside, so we have to move fast." He pulled out his gun. "You stay directly behind me. Okay?"

Serena nodded again, and when Cole signaled, she moved in behind him, as close as possible without touching.

They slipped up next to the craggy outcrop and climbed over, careful to be quiet. But rocks scattered and rolled in a small avalanche beneath her feet. She stifled a gasp as Cole's arm jutted out to keep her from falling. They advanced quickly and reached the entrance with no catastrophes. Cole listened, then they eased inside.

If she remembered correctly, this entrance was like the other, a narrow passage leading to another cavern, but with only one large side shaft like a tall train tunnel. It was braced on the sides with iron bars and wood beams, and metal tracks ran down the middle for the ore cars.

Ryan had always said he'd come back here, that someday he'd stick a pick into a vein of gold so thick he'd never have to work another day in his life.

Cole reached behind and grabbed her hand, then drew her with him as he inched forward.

Soon she discerned light, which she figured was the cavern ahead. Fright stabbed her. What if the guard started coming out while they were in here? What if the others returned?

Cole tightened his grip, and she was oddly reassured.

They stopped at the mouth of the inside cavern. A voice? Someone moaning.

Cole peered around the corner and saw the guard's back as he hovered over a limp form on the floor near the wall opposite them. The hostage the other guys had mentioned.

The guard handed a canteen to the hostage and said, "Drink, my friend."

The other man stretched out a wobbly arm and accepted whatever the guard was offering, but then flung it across the room. "Not your friend," he slurred.

The guard shrugged, then turned and started walking toward a large wooden box in the corner.

Cole motioned for Serena to stay put, held his gun at the ready and ran over to the guard, hoping surprise was in his favor. The man turned just as Cole threw a punch. The guy's eyes rolled upward and he went down and out. In seconds, Cole shoved the gun in his belt, then turned to help the hostage. As the man struggled to raise his head, Cole stopped dead. *Ryan.*

Cole jostled him. Damn, he was drugged. By choice or force, Cole didn't know. He picked up the canteen and poured some in Ryan's face, then started untying the rope around his legs.

No way could they get him out unless Ryan could move on his own. Just then Cole felt Serena's warmth behind him.

"We better hurry," she said. Then she spotted Ryan and her face went white. "Oh, God." She knelt and began helping Cole untie him.

Ryan mumbled, "Serena?"

Cole turned and handed her the rope. "Tie that guy's feet together."

As she did, Cole slipped off his belt to strap the guard's hands to one of the steel rebars, then he removed his bandanna and stuffed it in the guy's mouth. At that moment, voice echoed from the entrance.

On instinct, Cole shoved Serena ahead of him and into the tunnel. "Run."

She looked at Ryan. "But—"

"You go. I'll help him."

CHAPTER SIXTEEN

SERENA IGNORED THE order and reached to help Ryan up.

He accepted her hand, but couldn't quite grasp it. "Serena. I knew you'd find me."

Cole put one of Ryan's arms around his shoulder and Serena did the same. Then they all but dragged Ryan into the tunnel. She gulped air, and felt the pressure of Cole's hand on hers around Ryan's back. She felt his strength pulling both her and Ryan forward faster.

She didn't know who was following them, but figured it was the men she'd seen earlier.

"How far to the end?" Cole queried.

"Too far."

"Here, take the flashlight," he said. "I may have to stop to hold them off while you go ahead for help."

A harsh voice bellowed from somewhere behind them, sending another shard of fear through her.

More voices. But she couldn't make out anything being said.

Her heart thudded. The tunnel was cool, humid and dark; the only light was the swath cut by the flashlight. But they kept moving forward.

"There's a different way," Ryan suddenly said. "Up ahead. I found it earlier. It's shorter."

She felt Cole's hand fall away from hers. "You guys go on."

"No," she said, and grabbed Cole's hand. "We're not leaving Ryan. He said there's another way." At that, she felt Ryan stand without her support. He shoved both Cole and Serena ahead.

"Keep going," he said. "Trust me."

Fear the likes of which she'd never felt gripped her.

"You're trapped! Come out now," someone shouted.

She almost stopped to see if Ryan was okay, but he kept shoving her forward, propelling her faster. Cole pulled her behind him.

They rounded a curve, and the tunnel got lighter. She could actually see. Then Cole stopped short. He looked, listened. Serena listened, too, then heard a dull roar, which grew louder and louder. "What's that?"

Their eyes locked. "It sounds like a train,"

she said, realizing suddenly that the tracks under her feet vibrated like an earthquake registering six on the Richter scale.

"It's an underground river," Ryan said. "But the other tunnel is right ahead."

Cole yanked her forward again and the roar continued to increase, until it sounded as if they were standing under Niagara Falls. She held Cole's hand as in a vise; her feet were pounding as fast as her heart was hammering. Oh, God!

Cole halted abruptly and she did, too.

"Go to the left," Ryan said. "The tunnel is right there."

Serena looked left and saw a pinpoint of light in the distance. "C'mon," she said, and started forward, then stopped when she saw the ground in front had turned into a ledge and there was water below. In order to get out, they'd have to walk along the ledge for a few feet. She turned to Cole. "Are you still afraid of heights?"

"Get going," he said. He jerked his hand from hers and she dropped the flashlight. The deafening roar of the water enveloped her.

She drew in a deep breath, flattened herself against the wall and took a step. Then another and another. Cole and Ryan were right behind her. Then the ledge opened out, and the light in front of them grew more pronounced. Relief flooded her.

Cole stroked her back. "Keep moving."

She did, and in a few more feet, the path widened and they were all standing next to one another. "You think we lost them?"

Cole shot her a quick grin. "I think we did." He gave Ryan a playful tap on the arm. "Good work, Ry."

Just as he said it, Serena heard voices again. Her heart leaped to her throat. Where to go? She glanced around, and spotted another tunnel opposite them.

"Move," Ryan said.

Voices again. Closer.

She barreled ahead, with Cole and Ryan right behind. Ahead, bright white light glared, guiding her path. Once at the opening, she stopped and let her eyes adjust to the light outside. That was when she saw they stood on a bluff overlooking a lake. With nowhere to go but down. She clutched the cold wet granite behind her, fingernails scraping against the smooth surface.

"What now?"

"We jump," Ryan said.

She looked at Cole. He shrugged. "I'm the one afraid of heights. I'll follow you."

Her gaze darted back to the tunnel. Something shiny glinted. A flashlight? Or the barrel of a gun? Blood thundered in her ears.

Cole tipped his head forward, indicating she should jump.

Serena drew her lips between her teeth and bit down so hard the coppery taste of blood burst onto her tongue.

"It's the only way," Ryan said. "Let's go. It's a piece of cake."

Cole nudged her and held out his hand. "C'mon. We'll go together."

"I'll go first," Ryan quickly said, "and you'll see it's okay." With that, he pushed off from the wall and jumped into the open air.

Shaking like a leaf, she stared at Cole's outstretched hand. She placed her hand in his, and when he wrapped his fingers around hers, she nodded, and they both pushed off and plummeted into the void below.

White light turned black, and she felt as though she was floating in space. But she wasn't dead. She lost Cole's hand when they hit water. Down and down she went, until her fierce kicking sent her soaring to the surface, where she gasped for air.

Cole popped up nearby, surfacing with a giant splash. She paddled toward him, sucking in huge gulps of air. When Cole saw her, a giant smile creased his face.

Ryan paddled over then. "See," he said, his eyes still red. "Piece of cake."

Treading water, they all squinted toward the top of the escarpment. She couldn't believe she'd actually jumped—and not died.

"Yeah, piece of cake." She splashed a handful of muddy water at her brother.

"Hey watch it. Just because you're already wet doesn't mean you can't get dunked." They all laughed.

She should be exhausted, but instead, she was pumped. Ryan had really come through. She didn't know what was going on with those men, but Ry had come through.

She tipped her head back to swish the hair from her eyes, then she glanced around to see how far they had to swim to dry ground. As much as she liked water, she'd had her fill.

To their right was a stand of tall sycamore trees—an oasis in the middle of granite and sand. Cole looked in the same direction.

"Shoes off," he said. "Easier to swim that way."

She agreed, and when she finished removing her boots, he grabbed them, tied the laces and draped them around his neck. "Let's get out of here." He shot her a killer smile.

Serena launched off on her own, saying over her shoulder, "I'll race you guys." She thought she heard Cole snort, and in the next instant he was stroking past her. With each stroke, she regretted having opened her big mouth. Her clothes created resistence she hadn't counted on. And though she was mentally psyched, she was so physically exhausted, she was lucky if she'd be able to dog-paddle. Ryan was nearly at shore.

Cole, apparently seeing her struggle, treaded water to wait for her. "You can hold on to me if you want."

Suddenly, she wanted that more than she'd ever wanted anything. For once in her life, she wanted to depend on someone else, have a strong shoulder to lean on when she needed to.

It was almost tragic that the someone she wanted this from was Cole. She kept on swimming. "No, thank you. I might not be ready for the Olympics, but I'm sure I can make it on my own."

"Okay. Don't say I didn't offer," he said, then swam alongside. As they closed the gap between water and land, Cole tested the water's depth, and stood when it was knee deep. He held out his hand and drew Serena close to him.

She staggered, uneasy on her feet. Again she wanted to grab him, hold on and never let go. But he'd started sloshing to shore, where Ryan sat. She followed behind Cole, tired and drawing air from the bottom of her lungs as they reached dry ground and headed toward the stand of trees.

Serena had gone but a few steps when a woman emerged from behind a giant sycamore, a gun pointed directly at them.

Lucy.

In the next instant, Cole shoved Serena behind him, acting as her shield. "I don't know why you have that gun on us," Cole said quickly. "The only reason we're here is that we were looking for Ryan."

She stepped out from behind Cole. "Lucy, what's going on?"

Her brother came up beside them. "Put the gun down, Lucy. You're just going to get us in bigger trouble."

Serena stared at Ryan. "What's going on, Ryan?" She looked at Cole, then back to her brother, hoping neither would make a stupid move they'd regret later.

Carrying some kind of backpack, Lucy held the weapon steady while she pulled out a satellite phone, punched a button and started talking. "I need backup ASAP," she said, then gave whomever it was directions to their location. Serena heard her mention some names, apparently telling the others how to find them. When she hung up, she said, "Your sister wants to know what you're doing here, Ryan. Tell her."

He glanced away. "I didn't know what they were doing."

Serena's stomach knotted, anger and fear warring inside her. Instantly, she decided on a different tactic. "Thanks a lot, Ryan. I should have realized you'd screw up again. We nearly died back there. I think we deserve a better explanation than that." She intentionally raised her voice.

Ryan stared at her as though she were crazy and she winked almost imperceptibly.

He must've got it because he edged closer. "You should have known? Yeah, you should have known. Because that's what you think of me. I'm just a screwup." He walked over and got directly in Serena's face.

"Hey," Lucy said. "Stop that."

"Stop nothing. You know what she's like, Lucy. Always butting in, trying to run my life."

Lucy appeared confused and started to say something, but Ryan suddenly lurched to the side and grabbed the gun barrel.

In one swift instant, Lucy elbowed Ryan in the gut, grabbed his arm and threw him to the ground, facedown in the sand.

"Dammit, Ryan," Lucy said. "Don't try to be a hero here."

Ryan stood up, an uncertain smile on his face. "Jeez, Lucy. Where'd you learn that stuff?"

Serena stood with her mouth agape.

"Put your shoes on," Lucy said.

Cole's eyes narrowed and Serena had the feeling he was strugging to figure something out. All she wanted was to get them all out of there safely. Serena whirled, took her hiking boots from around Cole's neck and went to the tree. She plopped down in the sand underneath and jammed her feet into her boots. Cole came over, sat next to Serena and pulled on his own boots.

Ryan hadn't taken off his boots, but came over to stand in the shade next to them, bouncing from one foot to the other. She realized the drugs must have worn off and he was so tightly wound he could freak out at any minute. She didn't know what was going on, but whatever he'd agreed to with Lucy was bad, and they needed to get out of there before anyone else showed up. "Where's your car, Ryan?"

"That way." Ryan indicated with a nod.

"Get up and start walking," Lucy said. She tipped her head in the same direction Ryan had. "When you reach Ryan's car, get the hell out of here."

Cole, Serena and Ryan exchanged surprised glances. She was letting them go? Maybe she really did have feelings for Ryan. But the reason didn't matter. Serena and Cole started off and within seconds, Ryan followed. Serena had the distinct impression that Ryan had second thoughts about leaving Lucy there by herself.

The sun pounded mercilessly on their heads as they picked their way through a half mile of rocks. When they rounded the next hill and saw a beat-up, green camouflage Humvee parked in the shade of a scrub paloverde tree, Serena breathed a sigh of relief. The front of the vehicle had a roof over the top, but the back was open. There seemed to be some kind of tarp over whatever was in the rear. "It's not mine," Ryan said. "They had me drive it out here."

"What?"

Serena brushed sweat from her face. "God, it's an oven out here," she said. "I suddenly feel like I'm burning up." She glanced at Cole. "How're you doing?"

Cole touched her forehead. Her face was as red as an apple and she looked about to faint. "Get in the shade," he ordered, nudging her toward a paloverde tree. "She's gotta go back now!" he yelled at Ryan. Heatstroke was all too common in the desert and would sneak up on a person before he knew what hit him, and then it was too late.

He walked with her to make sure she was settled under the tree.

Ryan rummaged in the car again, then brought a canteen of water over to them. Cole grabbed it, spilled a little on his hands, patted Serena's forehead and cheeks with his damp fingertips and lifted the container to her lips. Even the water was boiling hot.

Ryan peered into Serena's eyes. "Serena? You okay?"

"I'm fine," she repeated, "and we have to call the sheriff again."

"I will," Cole said. He turned to Ryan, unapologetic. "We can drive to my car and I'll take Serena back in that." He was offering Ryan the opportunity to ditch the Humvee with whatever cargo was in the back. Cole had a pretty good idea what it was.

Ryan nodded.

"Give me your keys. I'll start the air."

Hesitant, Ryan got more water and handed his keys to Cole. Cole slid inside and jammed the key into the ignition, trying not to touch anything.

The Humvee started instantly. Once Cole got the air cranking, he sank in the seat, lowered his head and searched for a phone. Relief kicked in when he located a satellite phone under the seat, the kind used in the military, which should work almost anywhere. When he got a dial tone, he punched in 911. No sooner had he done so than Ryan sidled up to him.

Cole didn't know what Ryan might do if he knew the police might be on their way. He could panic and do something stupid. Ryan's judgment right now was questionable at best. If Ryan was going to be in trouble, he'd have to deal with it.

"Does it work?" Ryan asked.

"Seems to, but I can't get a stable connection to actually make a call," he lied. Cole set the phone back where he'd found it, shook his head and exited the vehicle.

Serena seemed to be resting comfortably now that she was out of the sun and had had some water. He surveyed the area, and decided they weren't too far from the road they'd come in on. One thing he knew with certainty was that whatever those guys were doing, it wasn't safe, and there was no telling how they'd react once the police got into the act.

"So what's your involvement in this?" Cole asked Ryan.

Ryan closed his eyes for a moment. "I just wanted to make some money. I—I thought I could do it just once and that would be it." He rubbed a hand over his face. "I didn't know that once you got in, you couldn't get out."

Cole bit the side of his cheek as he glanced at Serena. "So, what happens now?"

Ryan raked a hand through his hair. "I don't know. If I'm caught with this stuff I'll go to jail, and if I don't deliver, those guys will kill me…"

Cole realized he couldn't worry about Ryan. There was only one way he'd ever be able to live with himself again. "Well, I'm going to put Serena into that vehicle over there, and I'm going to drive her to safety. If you want to come along, that's fine with me."

CHAPTER SEVENTEEN

SERENA STARED AT COLE. Ryan was in the backseat, his head in his hands. Knowing how much trouble Ryan was in, she had no clue what to do. If Cole went to the police, she wasn't sure what would happen to Ryan.

It would take them a few hours to get back, she decided, and maybe during that time she could convince Cole that going to the police wasn't the best option. Ryan might be screwed up, but she knew in her heart he'd never hurt anyone. Cole stomped on the gas, and even with her seat belt on, she bounced up and down. She turned to look behind and saw two big Humvees cresting the hill bearing down on them. She motioned to Cole.

"Where the hell did they come from?" Cole shouted as he maneuvered over the rocky terrain.

Serena looked at Ryan, who was crouched over. "Ryan," she said, and poked him on the back. "Why are they after us?"

He gazed at her. "Oh, God. They want what's in the back."

She turned to Cole. "What should we do?"

He swung a curve. "If they want the stuff, let's give it to them."

Serena nodded. "Good idea."

Though reluctant, Ryan nodded, then crawled into the back. Serena followed and between the two of them, they chucked box after box into the desert. As they were about to toss the last one, Cole noticed one of the vehicles had stopped. But the other kept on. Shit.

"Oh, man," Ryan said. "I am so screwed."

Serena took a deep breath. "Do the right thing, Ryan, and I'll help you whatever way I can. The best lawyer, therapy, whatever. You can make this right, Ryan."

"What do you want to do, Ryan?" Cole continued in the same soothing tone. He was afraid Ryan would do something stupid and endanger all their lives. But maybe Ryan's feelings for Serena would kick in.

"Make a deal with the authorities and you'll get off easy. We'll testify on your behalf." He waited a few minutes for the message to sink in. "We're all willing to stand by you, and that will mean a lot to the court."

Faint sirens sounded, then got louder, and

Cole saw a half-dozen police vehicles come over the rise.

Suddenly sober, Ryan faced Serena. “Okay. I’ll do whatever I have to do.”

Cole checked the rearview mirror and saw the chasers stop and retreat. He halted when two squad cars cruised up alongside. Four more zoomed past apparently to chase down the guys who’d been holding Ryan hostage.

In less than an hour, they were all on their way out of there, Ryan in one squad car, Cole and Serena with Karl in another.

Cole asked Karl if he’d take him to his Jeep and Karl agreed.

Four hours later, he and Serena were together again sitting across from each other outside the interrogation room at the Prescott jail, which apparently had jurisdiction. The federal authorities had been called in, as well, since they were dealing with a large operation that smuggled firearms across the border into Mexico. Apparently the authorities had been on watch for a long time. And when Cole saw Lucy coming out of an interrogation room, his mouth dropped open.

“Lucy?” Serena asked. “What’s going on?”

Lucy looked amazingly different, Cole realized. Her hair was pulled back and the heavy makeup was gone. She walked over to

Serena and flashed a badge. "I'm sorry I couldn't say anything. I had no idea you'd go looking for Ryan. We've been on this case for nearly a year now."

Cole told his part of the story to the detectives, then came out and saw Serena lean her weary head against the wall. Her skin was tanned and freckled and sunburned all at the same time; her hair hung wild like a rustic frame around her delicate face. Her lips were dry and her eyes had purple smudges underneath; her clothes were caked with dust.

She was the most beautiful woman he'd ever seen. The women talked some more, but got quiet so Cole couldn't decipher what they were saying. He had a feeling it was about Ryan and what was going to happen.

He sat down beside Serena when Lucy left. "It's over," he said. "We can get on with our lives. Maybe—"

She halted him. Looked him in the eye. "No, it's not over, Cole. I have something else to tell you. Something I should have told you a long time ago."

Cole nodded. "Okay, but I have to point out, nothing that happened back then is going to affect anything. I'm through living my life based on the past."

Serena took a breath. *Easy to say.* "I have to

say this quickly, Cole, so if you cannot ask questions until I'm done, I'd really appreciate it."

He nodded again.

"One of the reasons I was so devastated by what happened on the night of our graduation was that I had something to tell you. Something I was excited about and was going to tell you when you returned." Unable to gaze at him, she kept her focus on her hands, which lay in her lap. "I was going to tell you I was pregnant."

Cole didn't move, then abruptly he shifted position to face her. "What?"

She held up a trembling hand. She had to just say it and say it all. "I was six weeks pregnant that night, and after the accident and learning you had been with Ginny, I was beside myself. I didn't know what to do. Ryan was going through hell thinking he was going to lose one of his legs, there was the funeral for Celine, everything was in chaos and I didn't know how long you'd be in jail, and all I could think was that I'd have to bring our baby to see you in jail. Aware how I felt having to do that with my own dad, I was horrified. I didn't know what to do or how to deal with any of it. My mom wasn't there for support, and in the end, I did what I thought was best for the baby. I gave him up for adoption."

Turning to Cole, she saw a look of disbelief

in his eyes. She bit back the sobs that threatened. "I—I'm sorry, Cole. You were in jail and it looked like it would be for a long time and there was no reason to tell you once I made that decision. I married Brett three months after giving the baby away. I was horribly depressed and needed someone to keep me from jumping off a bridge. He was willing, unfortunately for him. It was bad, and we knew just a few weeks into the marriage that it wasn't going to work."

He was still staring at her in disbelief, then, slowly, hurt filled his eyes, which were suddenly clouded with tears. She turned away, unable to bear his pain.

"You gave away our child?" He said the words so softly she almost didn't hear him. "How could you do that? How could you not tell me? I could have raised him if you didn't want him." He shook his head. "All this time I've had a son. You not only deprived me of him, but even the knowledge of him. How could you do that?"

Oh, God. Her throat closed and she could barely get out the words. "It wasn't that simple. I wasn't thinking of you, I wasn't thinking of me. I was thinking of our child and what kind of life he'd have with a mother who couldn't support him and a father in jail. I had no one there to help me make the decision, and I did what I thought was best." She took a deep breath. "And just like you, there's not a day that goes by that I don't think of it and wonder what life would be like if I'd made a different decision. But I didn't. And I have to live with it. There didn't seem to be any point in telling you because what was done was done."

He was quiet for the longest time, then finally said, "So, why are you telling me now?"

She took another breath. "What difference does it make?"

He shook his head resignedly. "None, I guess." Then he got up and walked away.

CHAPTER EIGHTEEN

"HEY THERE."

Serena snapped to attention when she heard Tori's voice. Then she saw Natalia, too. The two friends sat on either side of her. Serena opened her mouth to explain, but nothing came out.

"You don't have to say anything," Tori said. "We heard a lot on the news, and the rest can wait till later." She shrugged. "Or never."

Serena was glad her friends had come to pick her up at the Prescott Police Department since she had no car, but all she could think of was the look in Cole's eyes when she'd told him. That and the fear in Ryan's.

Gazing at her friends, she said, "I don't have any idea how long this will take. Why don't you go back and I'll figure out another way to get home."

"No," Natalia said. "You need us."

Serena couldn't help smiling. "I know I do.

But sometimes, it's better to face the demons alone. I have to do some real soul-searching."

Her friends exchanged glances.

"Okay," Natalia said. "We respect that. But remember, you aren't the bad guy. Ryan's his own person. He makes his own decisions. People make decisions they think are right at the time. In the end, there is no right or wrong. Just what's right at the time for that person."

"Thanks," Serena said.

Just then a detective emerged and motioned for her to accompany him.

"We'll be waiting at the nearest coffee shop," Tori said. "Call me when you're done."

Serena smiled, but her heart wasn't in it. "What would I do without you guys?"

She followed the detective to his desk in a large open room with three other desks. Cole sat with another detective in the corner across from her.

Oh, God. She lowered her head, unable to even look at him.

COLE FINISHED WITH THE detective, then moved like an automaton in an effort to get away. He went into the men's room, propped himself against the wall and closed his eyes. He'd had to call up every ounce of willpower not to scream. He couldn't even begin to digest what Serena had told him. A child.

They'd had a child. A little boy. And she'd never said a word. All these years he'd been a father. The father of a child who was out there somewhere, believing another man was his father.

Tears gathered behind his eyelids. Anger coiled in his belly. God, how could their lives get so fricking screwed up?

If he'd only known. Hell, he couldn't even imagine what their child might look like. Did the boy have a lot of hair like him? Brown eyes like Serena? Red hair, or even dark like her brother? Was he shy or outgoing? Have big hands like Cole, or long slender fingers like Serena?

Suddenly, he felt a sense of loss that he'd only felt once before when his beloved grandmother had died. The worst part wasn't that he'd been denied the chance to love his son; it was the thought that if Serena had told him she was pregnant in the beginning, when she first learned about it, their lives would have been entirely different. They would have been a family.

Why had she waited to tell him?

He'd no sooner thought it then he realized how horrible the loss had to be for Serena. She'd carried the baby in her body for nine months, gone through labor and then had given him up. He couldn't imagine what that might be like. His only consolation was in knowing that his little boy had been well loved during that time—of that he was certain.

He went to the sink and splashed cold water on his face. But he couldn't go out there and see Serena again. His thoughts spiraled. He'd have to tell his mother. She deserved to know she'd been a grandmother. No…she *was* a grandmother. Still.

He came out of the john, but instead of going back to where Serena was, he found a bench halfway down the hall, with a door between them.

Five minutes later, Detective Millford walked out with Serena and said, "You both look like you might want to get out of here and get a good night's sleep. As soon as I've filled out some forms for you to sign, we'll be done and you can go."

Serena nodded, then glanced at Cole. She gazed at him a long while, then turned and went away.

He sat there for the longest time, not wanting to think about everything that had happened, yet unable to think about anything else. How had he gotten so involved? Did he still love Serena, or was everything he was feeling born of their shared history?

Just then, Ryan appeared with an officer, went over and said something to Serena, then left again. Cole's stomach tightened just seeing

Ryan. He didn't deserve Serena's loyalty, and he hoped she didn't keep getting sucked in.

For Cole, the problem was just the opposite. He *was* to blame for everything that had happened to him. Hell, realistically, he couldn't even blame Serena for making the choice that she had.

Still, it hurt like hell.

A WEEK HAD GONE BY since their desert escapade and Serena felt still in a daze. She went through each day by rote. Open the shop, greet people with her fake smile, close the shop, prepare for the next day. She hadn't seen Ryan since that night because he'd been taken to the jail to be fingerprinted, and then they'd put him in isolation, since he was working on a plea bargain with state and federal authorities. She'd promised her brother she'd get him an excellent attorney, and she'd already called Tori's uncle, Charlie, who said it didn't look good. Ryan might still end up in prison, and with his temperament, she worried he probably wouldn't last a day before he got someone ticked off.

After what had happened, she had to face some hard facts. What Cole had said was exactly right. She had known it all along, but she hadn't been able to make the break. Ryan could be right, too. All the help she'd given might have been to assauge her own guilt. She'd always been smarter than Ryan, things had come easy to her, and she'd felt guilty about it. Ryan had taken advantage of her guilt, she realized. Beyond that, she was stricken with remorse. Cole had asked why she'd told him now, and she'd had to hold herself back from saying because she loved him. And because he deserved to know. It was his right.

She almost laughed. She and Ryan were *both* totally screwed up.

Deciding against a shower, she drew a bath, took off her clothes and sank into the warm water, letting it envelop her, comfort her. But her thoughts kept her on edge.

She couldn't leave Ryan to face a trial all alone; she had to be supportive. Supportive, but not codependent, she reminded herself.

She still couldn't fathom all the people involved in the drug and weapons bust, yet it seemed only the little guys had been arrested.

More disconcerting was that suddenly, without Ryan around, her life seemed incredibly empty. Yes, she still had friends and the café, and people were friendly and came in all the time, but her life didn't feel the same. And she didn't know why.

Or had it always been like this and she'd just convinced herself that having a home—having roots—was synonymous with security? Was that it? Maybe security was something you had to achieve internally. Maybe her longing for security didn't have anything to do with where she lived or how she conducted her personal life.

She knew the answer to that, too. The ultimate security was not just trusting yourself, but also in giving your trust to another. She'd never done that. Not even with Cole. The man she still loved. How was she ever going to reconcile that?

The day after Ryan's hearing, Brody had wanted to visit to console her. She'd told him no, of course, and he'd taken it badly, saying he'd give her time and call again. But she didn't need time and told him so.

When she finished her bath, she put on some sweats, went downstairs and started preparing the espresso maker for the next day. She was supposed to see Isabella after she closed the café, supposedly to talk about the business since Ryan was indisposed. She didn't know if Cole had told her about the baby, but she had to expect that he had.

COLE PACED THE KITCHEN, waiting for his mom. A week and a half had passed since everything had happened. A week and a half since he'd seen or talked with Serena.

Her brother was going to get a better deal than he deserved, and the rest of the guys would be in jail for a long time. They'd had the book thrown at them.

He hadn't told his mother about her grandchild yet, but he planned to. She was probably the only person who might understand how he felt. Even though Cole's dad had left, his mother had kept him, raised him alone, and he couldn't imagine that she'd even contemplated doing something different.

He was about to go and find his mom, when she walked into the room. The past week she seemed to be getting cheerier and cheerier. "Hi, Mom. Sit down. I have something I want to speak to you about."

"If it's about talking to Serena about the business, she'll be here very shortly."

He nodded. "Good. That's good. How is she doing?"

"Okay, I guess. We didn't talk, figuring it could wait until today." She turned sharply to look at him. "Why do you want to know?"

He held out a chair for her. "Coffee's made. I'll get you a cup."

"Serena still cares about you, you know."

"What? Why on earth would you say that?"

"I saw her reaction when your name cropped up."

Cole's gut wrenched. "Believe me, the last person she cares about is me. In fact, I've got to tell you something important, and it has to do with Serena."

He made sure his mother was comfortable, poured her a cup of coffee with milk in it and one for himself. Then he sat and told her the whole story. Oddly, his mom didn't seem surprised.

"So now you hate her for thinking about the child and not you?" his mom said.

"I don't hate her. I just can't forgive her. I never got to see him. Never got to touch him. Do you know how that makes me feel? You had a grandson you never saw. Doesn't that make you sad? It does me. It makes me very sad." And angry. He felt his nerves tense every time he thought about it.

"You're blaming the wrong person, Cole. People do things they believe are right. Maybe they find out later that they're wrong, but sometimes you can't fix it. You should learn to forgive if you expect people to forgive you."

He shoved back his chair and stood. "I don't expect forgiveness. I know what I did, and I deserve whatever people want to feel about it. This is different."

"Oh? Why is it different?"

"It's different because someone took something from me. Just like my dad. I had nothing to say about that, either. He left and you decided never to tell me who he was. I resent that. I always have. I forgive you, but I resent it."

She moistened her lips. "I know. And I'm sorry. I kept it from you because I was trying to do the right thing by you."

"How is it right to keep my father's identity a secret? I deserve to know, don't I?"

"I love you. I didn't want to hurt you."

He sat back down, not understanding anything at all. "Why don't you just tell me and let me be the judge."

Closing her eyes, she inhaled, as if bracing herself to do something horrible.

"It can't be that bad. He can't have been that horrible, not if you loved him," Cole said.

"That's the problem, Cole. I didn't love him. I didn't even know him."

"What?" He pulled back. "I don't understand."

"No," she said, shaking her head. "I didn't know him. A man I was seeing… He was married, and when he broke off with me, I couldn't stand it. One night a few months later, I felt so lonely I went to a bar in Phoenix and was with someone. I never saw him after that. I never even knew his name. And I got pregnant."

Cole felt his mouth fall open. The air squeezed from his lungs. He heard a faint noise somewhere in the background, but all he could focus on was what his mother had said.

She bowed her head, and her shoulders sagged when she added, "I thought it was better for you not to know. I still think I was right not to tell you. But it's been a burden to carry all these years. I'm sure Serena's felt that kind of burden, as well."

He had no response. None whatsoever.

Then he realized the noise he'd heard was someone at the door. But he didn't want to see anyone.

A voice rang out. "Isabella? Are you here?"

Serena.

"Yes, just a moment," his mom said.

His head throbbed, and he stalked past Serena and sprinted out of the house.

"I'M SORRY," SERENA SAID. "I didn't mean to interrupt anything. I've brought some leftover scones."

Bella waved a hand. "He's just upset."

Serena could only imagine. "Did…did he tell you what happened?"

She nodded. "He told me about the baby."

Oh, God. But she figured he would, and in a way she was glad. She was tired of carrying such a heavy burden. Now that it wasn't a secret anymore, maybe she could get on with her life. Whatever that was. "I'm sorry," she said. "I don't know what to say except that I was young and I thought I was doing the right thing."

Bella smiled. "I know. I think you did, too."

Incredulous, Serena wasn't sure she'd heard her right. "What did you say?"

"The decision had to be a tough one to make," she said. "Cole just needs to learn how to forgive. Even himself."

Serena knew better than anyone how hard it was.

"I don't believe he can ever do that," Serena said. She'd listened to him, saw the pain in his eyes.

"He's so hard on himself, and I wish I could help him, but I can't."

Serena stopped and took out her wallet. "Here, I want you and Cole to have this." She removed a photo, one she'd sneaked before they'd taken her baby away. "It's not much to hang on to, but it's something. I always hold out the hope that one day, maybe he'll want to find out who his biological parents are. But if he never does, at least I'm comforted in knowing he has had a better life than he would have had with just me."

CHAPTER NINETEEN

THREE WEEKS LATER, Serena lowered herself into the easy chair next to the window at the Purple Jeep Touring Company. Too nervous to sit, she stood again, parted the blinds and stared out at the crimson mountains in the background.

Like a movie backdrop, she thought. Surreal, almost. Puffy white clouds hung like giant cotton balls in a clear blue sky. Bright green pine trees and juniper dotted the landscape, a vivid contrast with the red rock.

She was taking control, and that was that.

"Okay. Sorry about that," Cole said, reentering the room while slipping his arms into a white safari shirt. "I've got a tour in ten minutes." He continued buttoning his shirt.

"I'll only be a minute." One minute in which she couldn't drag her gaze away from his bare chest. "I came to thank you for all that you've done for Ryan."

His feet were bare, and he worked the rug

underneath them with his toes. “No need to thank me. I owe him a lot more.”

“Well, your testimony made everything a lot easier.”

“Lucy…I mean Detective Sanchez’s testimony helped even more,” Cole said.

She swallowed. This was so hard, but she’d had to do it. It was the only way to free herself…and him. She stood to face him. “I also came here to tell you I forgive you.”

His head shot up.

“I’ve spent a lot of time living in the past, and I can’t do it anymore. I know you didn’t do anything intentionally. You were a teenager who made a bad decision. I also want you to know I didn’t do what I did because I hated you or was trying to get even. I loved you, and even though I thought you’d put your friends before me, I got over that. I made a mistake, too, in not telling you about the baby. I realize that now. But that’s not all of why I’m here. I need to tell you that I hope and pray someday you’ll be able to forgive yourself.”

A panoply of emotions played over his face. Surprise, puzzlement, acute pain. “Serena, you did what you believed was right. I understand that. What hurts, and what I don’t understand is why you got involved with me again…when we were out looking for Ryan.”

She raised a hand to her throat. "I got involved for the same reason I told you about the baby. I love you. I've never stopped loving you." She took a deep breath. As long as it was truth time, she might as well say it all. "And I wanted desperately to believe that was why you were with me, too. But delusion only lasts a little while." She gave a wan smile, trying to make light.

For the longest time, he simply stood there, shirttails hanging out, both hands at his waist. He stared past her, out the window, then walked over and locked the door.

Then he turned, took her firmly by the arms, sat her in one of the chairs and sat down across from her. He leaned toward her, his eyes meeting hers.

"What happened between us meant more to me than you can imagine—back in high school and now. But I know how hard being me in this town is and—"

Serena lifted a hand to stop him. Her throat cramped. None of that mattered. What mattered was what was in her heart…and his. She stood up, stepped to the window and gazed out. "I made some decisions in the past couple days. I decided I had to be honest and tell you how I feel. And after that, I just have to let us go and move on."

"Move on?" Cole spat. "Serena, this might sound strange, but believe it or not, I know who I am. I know why I'm doing what I am with my life. Except for one thing."

"One thing?"

"Yes. When I was a kid," Cole said, "I'd lie awake at night and get stomach cramps wondering why my dad didn't care enough about me to even stick around. And I was always feeling sorry for my mom because it hurt her that he'd left and it was so hard for her to just keep food on the table."

He sucked in a breath. "I spent my whole life worrying and wondering about something that didn't amount to anything in the end. My dad didn't leave. My mother had never told him about me. The fact was, she didn't even know him. So now I think about all that lost time and how pointless it was. I don't want to do that anymore. And I realized that although I came back because of my mother, I also came back because I needed answers, and I knew this was the only place I'd get them. I wanted answers from you. Now I know even that was wrong. You did whatever you did for your own reasons."

"The wrong reasons."

"No, not wrong. They were right at the time, and that's where we have to leave it. We're living in the now, not in the past."

He was so close his warm breath fanned her face when he spoke. Then, tentative, unsure, he reached out, his fingertips barely touching hers. He lifted her hand and placed it over his heart, pressing both his hands over hers.

"You're in my heart, Serena. You've always been there and always will be."

As she heard the catch in his voice, tears welled in her eyes. A river of emotion suddenly flowed between Cole and her, the current swift and powerful.

"I'm willing to take a chance if you are," he said gently.

Serena's heart filled with love and joy and she knew right then and there that not only was she willing, she was ready to take that chance. Yet it wasn't a chance at all. Her love for Cole was as certain as anything she'd ever known to be true.

"But there are no guarantees that—"

Serena cut him off with a fingertip to his lips. "I love you, Cole." Softly, she traced a line along his jaw. "I love you with all my heart."

Pure, impossible joy coursed through Cole, reaching all the empty places inside. "And I love you, Serena Matlock. More than I ever thought possible."

* * * * *

Celebrate Harlequin's 60th anniversary with Harlequin® Superromance® and the DIAMOND LEGACY *miniseries!*

Follow the stories of four cousins as they come to terms with the complications of love and what it means to be a family. Discover with them the sixty-year-old secret that rocks not one but two families in...
A DAUGHTER'S TRUST
by Tara Taylor Quinn.

Available in September 2009 from Harlequin® Superromance®

RICK'S APPOINTMENT with his attorney early Wednesday morning went only moderately better than his meeting with social services the day before. The prognosis wasn't great—but at least his attorney was going to file a motion for DNA testing. Just so Rick could petition to see the child…his sister's baby. The sister he didn't know he had until it was too late.

The rest of what his attorney said had been downhill from there.

Cell phone in hand before he'd even reached his Nitro, Rick punched in the speed dial number he'd programmed the day before.

Maybe foster parent Sue Bookman hadn't received his message. Or had lost his number. Maybe she didn't want to talk to him. At this point he didn't much care what she wanted.

"Hello?" She answered before the first ring was complete. And sounded breathless.

Young and breathless.

"Ms. Bookman?"

"Yes. This is Rick Kraynick, right?"

"Yes, ma'am."

"I recognized your number on caller ID," she said, her voice uneven, as though she was still engaged in whatever physical activity had her so breathless to begin with. "I'm sorry I didn't get back to you. I've been a little…distracted."

The words came in more disjointed spurts. Was she jogging?

"No problem," he said, when, in fact, he'd spent the better part of the night before watching his phone. And fretting. "Did I get you at a bad time?"

"No worse than usual," she said, adding, "Better than some. So, how can I help?"

God, if only this could be so easy. He'd ask. She'd help. And life could go well. At least for one little person in his family.

It would be a first.

"Mr. Kraynick?"

"Yes. Sorry. I was… Are you sure there isn't a better time to call?"

"I'm bouncing a baby, Mr. Kraynick. It's what I do."

"Is it Carrie?" he asked quickly, his pulse racing.

"How do you know Carrie?" She sounded defensive, which wouldn't do him any good.

"I'm her uncle," he explained, "her mother's—Christy's—older brother, and I know you have her."

"I can neither confirm nor deny your allegations, Mr. Kraynick. Please call social services." She rattled off the number.

"Wait!" he said, unable to hide his urgency. "Please," he said more calmly. "Just hear me out."

"How did you find me?"

"A friend of Christy's."

"I'm sorry I can't help you, Mr. Kraynick," she said softly. "This conversation is over."

"I grew up in foster care," he said, as though that gave him some special privilege. Some insider's edge.

"Then you know you shouldn't be calling me at all."

"Yes… But Carrie is my niece," he said. "I need to see her. To know that she's okay."

"You'll have to go through social services to arrange that."

"I'm sure you know it's not as easy as it sounds. I'm a single man with no real ties and I've no intention of petitioning for custody. They aren't real eager to give me the time of day. I never even knew Carrie's mother. For all intents and purposes, our mother didn't raise either one of us. All I have going for me is half a set of genes. My lawyer's on it, but it could be weeks—months—before this is sorted out. Carrie could be adopted by then. Which would be fine, great for her, but then I'd have lost my chance. I don't want to take her. I won't hurt her. I just have to see her."

"I'm sorry, Mr. Kraynick, but…"

* * * * *

Find out if Rick Kraynick will ever have a chance to meet his niece.
Look for A DAUGHTER'S TRUST
by Tara Taylor Quinn,
available in September 2009.

Silhouette®

SPECIAL EDITION™

Emotional, compelling stories that capture the intensity of living, loving and creating a family in today's world.

Modern, passionate reads that are powerful and provocative.

Silhouette®

nocturne

Dramatic and sensual tales of paranormal romance.

Romances that are sparked by danger and fueled by passion.